The Savage Life

**Lock Down Publications and
Ca$h Presents**
The Savage Life
A Novel by J-Blunt

The Savage Life

Lock Down Publications
P.O. Box 870494
Mesquite, Tx 75187

Visit our website
www.lockdownpublications.com

Lock Down Publications
Like our page on Facebook: Lock Down Publications @
www.facebook.com/lockdownpublications.ldp
Cover design and layout by: **Dynasty Cover Me**
Book interior design by: **Shawn Walker**
Edited by: **Lauren Burton**

Stay Connected with Us!

Text **LOCKDOWN** to 22828 to stay up-to-date with new releases, sneak peeks, contests and more...

Submission Guideline.

Submit the first three chapters of your completed manuscript to ldpsubmissions@gmail.com, subject line: Your book's title. The manuscript must be in a .doc file and sent as an attachment. The document should be in Times New Roman, double-spaced and in size 12 font. Also, provide your synopsis and full contact information. If sending multiple submissions, they must each be in a separate email.

Have a story but no way to send it electronically? You can still submit to LDP/Ca$h Presents. Send in the first three chapters, written or typed, of your completed manuscript to:

LDP: Submissions Dept
Po Box 870494
Mesquite, Tx 75187

DO NOT send original manuscript. Must be a duplicate.

Provide your synopsis and a cover letter containing your full contact information.

Thanks for considering LDP and Ca$h Presents.

J-Blunt

Prologue

Knock, knock, knock!

"Ay, Dion! Get the door, nigga!" J-Mac called from the kitchen. He was surrounded by four young niggas, a pile of money on the floor in front of them. He shook the dice vigorously, planning to walk away with the money. Nothing would pull him away from the prize.

"Nigga, I'm busy! One of you niggas get it," Dion called from behind the closed door. He was in the room with Casci, a buss-it baby from the hood, and was about to set a record for getting a girl to undress the fastest. He didn't care if Trump was at the door. No way he was moving. Casci's tight, voluptuous body demanded his full attention.

"Broke-ass nigga!" J-Mac sulked, putting the dice game on hold. "That's why yo' bitch-ass ain't got no money now. Always choosin' pussy over paper. MOB, nigga!" he yelled as he passed the closed door.

MOB was a popular acronym most hustlers and street niggas quoted. Money Over Bitches. Plain and simple. And J-Mac was salty he had to put his money on hold while Dion tricked off with a bitch.

"Who dat?" he called when he neared the front door.

"Luna. Y'all got that icky?" a deep voice called from outside.

J-Mac racked his brain, trying to put a face with the name as he checked the peephole. A tall, light-skinned nigga wearing dark clothes stood on the porch. "Who sent you?"

"Isaiah said y'all got that bag."

Hearing the name made J-Mac smile. He met Isaiah five months ago when him and Dion first opened their trap house. They weren't from Milwaukee, so they found a native to the area to spread the word.

"C'mon in, dawg. Isaiah is my nigga," J-Mac said, opening the door. "What you need, my nigga?"

"Lemme get a half-zip of loud."

J-Mac smiled wider, his dark lips curling upward, revealing raggedy teeth. His big, fish-like eyes turning into greedy slits. The hustler was the furthest thing from handsome, but the money he amassed made him feel like a star. There was no such thing as ugly when you had money.

He went into his pocket and pulled out four baggies of lime green weed, handing them to his customer

"This shit that gas?" Luna asked, putting the bags to his nose and taking a big sniff.

"That right there is what them niggas be smokin' right before they pull a Jihad," J-Mac cracked.

"Oh, this that Bin Laden, huh? Shit niggas was smokin' on 9/11," Luna laughed.

"Straight from Afghanistan. Two hunnid a pop."

"Okay. I'ma probably be back before the night is over. Y'all still gon' be crackin'?"

"Fo' sho. We neva sleep or run out," J-Mack said.

After completing the transaction, Luna stepped onto the porch. "Okay, fam. Oh, and one more thing."

J-Mac paused, letting the door hang open, anticipating another sale. "'Sup?"

"Lay it down, bitch!" Luna yelled, spinning around and slapping J-Mac in the face with a chrome .45.

When the big silver pistol met his jaw, there was a loud crunch as he crumpled to the floor, clutching his battered face. He closed his eyes for a moment. When he opened them again, Luna and another nigga were running into the house with their guns drawn. Two more were running up on the porch, holding heat with extended clips. None of them wore masks.

When the young niggas shooting dice in the kitchen reached for their pistols, gunshots rang out, sounding like thunder.

Pop, pop, pop, pop, pop, pop, pop, pop, pop, pop, pop!"

Bodies jerked, falling to the ground. The ones that didn't get hit acted like they were shot, lying on the ground and not moving.

"Roll on you stomach, nigga!" a brown-skinned man with long braids ordered.

J-Mac did as he was told, burning Luna and his niggas' faces into his mind, keeping his hands in the open. If he survived this, the jackers and everybody they knew would be in body bags.

The hit took less than five minutes, the jackboys taking jewelry, guns, drugs, and money. J-Mac lay on the floor, watching as the jackers gathered all the loot. His eyes met Casci and Dion's. They lay on the floor next to him. She was crying, and Dion looked like he wanted to cry. Seeing the fear in their eyes pissed him off.

Then one of the jackers walked over to Dion and shot him in the back of the head. Another nigga did the same thing to Casci. J-Mac knew he was next and felt helpless.

The stick-up kid walked up to him and pressed the barrel into the side of his face and squeezed the trigger.

J-Blunt

Chapter 1

"Dro, where you at, nigga?"

"At my BM crib. Why you callin' so early, nigga?"

"We got a problem, my nigga. I'm on the way."

Click.

"What you mean we got a problem? Twenty?" When no one answered, he checked the screen and seen the call had ended. "Fuck!" he cursed, tossing the phone on the bed.

It was eight o'clock in the morning. He was hung over and tired as fuck. He didn't want to deal with any problems. Plus, their problems were never regular problems. Every problem Dro had as of late involved death, jail, or drama, and it was too early to be dealing with that shit.

"Bitch-ass shit!" the lanky 25-year-old cursed, glancing down at his baby mama. America was sprawled out in bed, snoring lightly, the sheet barely covering her big-ass booty. He wished he could still be asleep.

After climbing out of bed and throwing on a pair of shorts, he hit the bathroom to kill the monster in his mouth before peeking in the back room to check on his daughter, Asia. The eight-year-old was sleeping next to her cousin, Taeiana.

After closing the door, he went to the living room and plopped down on the couch, lighting the half of a blunt that was in the ashtray. The THC hit his lungs like a mac truck. Dro loved wake-up blunts. The weed seemed more potent after just opening his eyes.

While he toked away at the loud, he grabbed the remote and powered on the 42" TV on the wall. After flipping through the channels, he stopped when something caught his eye. T.D. Jakes. And the preacher was going off!

Dro was raised up going to church every Sunday, and although he was trapped in the street life, he loved God and loved hearing the word preached. He stopped whatever he was doing and tuned in. He believed God had a calling on his life, but the streets had a firm hold of him. And he would continue playing in the streets until God got his attention. So, while T.D. Jakes huffed and puffed about Jesus, he huffed and puffed on the blunt.

He had just tossed the roach in the ashtray when the doorbell rang. After checking the window, he smiled.

Twenty was a little brown-skinned nigga with long dreads. Standing five-foot-six and 150 pounds, the thirty-year-old looked like a boy. But what he lacked in height, he made up with heart and a quick trigger finger.

"What up, nigga?" Dro greeted after opening the door.

"It's all bad," Twenty fumed, stepping into the house.

Dro locked the door quickly and spun to face him. "What happened? Somebody get murked?"

Twenty slung a wayward dreadlock over his shoulder and let out a long breath. "Them niggas from that weed house lookin' for us. One of them niggas survived."

Dro closed his eyes for a moment, the reality of the situation setting in. "We gave all them niggas shots to the head. How the fuck they survive? And how they know who we is?"

"That bitch, Tulip."

The look on Dro's face told his disbelief. "You mean Isaiah bitch, Tulip?"

Twenty nodded. "Yeah, fam. Nigga ran his mouf."

"Fuck wrong wit' that nigga? He know the G Code. You neva tell yo' bitch what you doin' in the streets."

"And you ain't gon' believe what else."

Dro eyed his boy, wondering how the situation could get worse. "Don't tell me that nigga using that shit to try to get some more money?"

Twenty waved off his words. "Hell nah. I'da clapped up him and his bitch on sight if they'da tried that bitch-ass shit. It's worse. The nigga jaw that Lunatic broke is her baby daddy."

Dro's eyes got so wide it was hard to tell he just smoked some weed. "Brah, I shot that nigga in the face. Close range. Damn near burnt his shit with the barrel. How the fuck he survive? And why would that stupid-ass nigga Isaiah tell us to rob his girl baby daddy and then tell her about it?"

"I don't know. We can ask that nigga after we find him. But I know where that bitch at right now. Let's snatch that bitch and get her missing. She could point us out to them niggas, and we can't have that. All they know is we Savages, and I don't think they know where we from 'cause she don't. Knockin' her off could give us time to get them niggas before they hit us."

Dro looked unsure. "Damn, my nigga. These bodies startin' to add up. All this shit gon' put Twelve in the mix."

"Fuck that bitch. She one of them. If them niggas catch us, they ain't gon' be worried about the police. They shooting. And that bitch gotta go. Dead people can't talk."

Dro paused to mull it over, eventually realizing his nigga was right. "This shit fucked up. Let me go get dressed."

"Ay, fam! You watching T.D. Jakes?" Twenty yelled after his retreating back.

"Yeah. That's my dude. He be spittin' that fire."

"Smoking weed and watching church. The devil is a lie!" Twenty laughed.

Dro walked into the bedroom and began rummaging around to find clothes to wear. After slipping into a pair of dark jeans and a t-shirt, he walked in the closet to grab the Mac-11.

"Where you goin'?" America asked, sitting up in bed. Despite being half asleep and hung over, his baby momma was bad. She was a natural beauty with reddish-brown skin, brown eyes, and hair shaved on one side of her head while the rest hung past her shoulders.

"You worried about the wrong thing. Go back to sleep," he mumbled, checking the 32-shot clip.

"Don't go, Dro. I got a bad feeling about this one, baby."

He stopped what he was doing to mug her. One thing he hated was people speaking doom on a move he was about to make. She didn't know exactly what he did in the streets or how he made money, and he would never tell her the details. All she knew was he carried guns, wore vests, and had piles of money. Part of him believed she knew what he did in the streets. He hadn't had a dope sack in years, but she knew not to ask questions.

"What I tell you 'bout that shit?"

"I know you don't like it, but something don't feel right. I think you should sit this one out and chill with me and Asia."

He continued staring at her, thinking about what T.D. Jakes had just preached on TV about prophetic dreams and their warnings. Now America was talking about her 'bad feeling.' Was God trying to tell him something or get his attention? It wouldn't be the first time someone warned him about something he was about to do. But it could also be the weed making him paranoid. Either way, he had to shut up Tulip. If he didn't, him and his niggas could be on the end of some hot shit.

"I'ma holla at you later," he mumbled before leaving.

Outside, they hopped into one of Twenty's dummy cars, a maroon Mercury Sable with tinted windows. The car was unregistered and untraceable. Dro was the driver, heading to pick up another member of the Savages.

Tae was the oldest at 32. He stood five-foot-ten and 180 pounds, but carried himself like he was seven feet tall. The brown-skinned goon wore his hair in cornrows to the back, looking like mix between Snoop and NBA superstar Kawhi Leonard.

"'Sup wit' chu niggas? Where Luna at?" Tae asked, hopping in the back seat.

"I tried callin', but he ain't hit me back," Twenty said. "We gon' have to make the move without him."

"Nigga at Whisper house, laid up wit' them hoes," Dro added.

"Fuck it. Let's get this bitch. Find out what we can about her nigga and clap all they asses up."

Tulip worked at a telecommunications company on Milwaukee's north side. After pulling onto the property, Dro did a lap around the building so they could check for cameras or security. They didn't see either. After finding her car, they parked next to it and began the wait.

"You sure y'all didn't see no cameras?" Dro asked, being extra careful.

"We good, nigga," Twenty said. "I drove past on the way to yo' house. We gon' lamp on this bitch and get her fucked over."

"If that bitch scream or try to run, I'm banging that bitch right here. She ain't gettin' away," Tae said, eyeing the building's front doors.

"You know I don't give a fuck," Twenty laughed. "I think we should say fuck it and just push her shit back when she come out to her car."

"Calm y'all trigger-happy asses down," Dro spoke up. "We gotta find out who her nigga is first."

Twenty nodded. "I know, nigga. We just talking shit. I know the move."

They didn't have to wait long for the woman of the hour.

At 11:17 a short, slim woman with close-cropped hair walked out of the glass double doors of the telecommunications company. Alone.

The Savages checked the parking lot for potential witnesses. The coast looked clear.

She walked like she didn't have a care in the world, not paying attention to the maroon sedan as she searched her purse for car keys.

Twenty waited until she began unlocking the door before letting the window down. "Get in, bitch! And you betta not scream!" he ordered, pointing a .380 Smith and Wesson with an extended clip at her.

When she spun around and seen Twenty with the gun, her face turned pale like she'd seen a ghost. The fight or flight instinct passed through her mind. That's when Tae opened the back door, waving a big-ass Chrome .44 Magnum.

"Get in, bitch!"

One look at the hand cannon made her cooperate and get in the back seat. Dro drove away coolly, heading to the spot.

"You thought yo' baby daddy was gon' get us knocked off, huh?" Tae asked.

"I swear to God, I don't know what you talkin' 'bout," she cried.

"She lyin', fam. Smack that bitch!" Twenty cheered.

Smack!

"Ahh!"

"Shut yo' lyin' ass up, bitch!" Tae yelled. pulling out a Taser. "Who them niggas lookin' for us? And where they be at?"

"I don't know what you talking about."

"Bitch, you still lyin'? Shock that bitch!" Twenty said.

"Ahh! Please, stop! I wasn't gon' let them kill y'all. I swear to God!"

Tae Tased her again.

"Ahh!"

"Tell me where them niggas be at," he ordered, resting the Taser at her throat.

"I-I-I," she stuttered.

"Ahh!"

Dro pulled up to a stop sign, ears ringing from Tulip's screams. He was about to tell Tae to stop shocking her, but a police car blew through the stop sign to the left, speeding past, the sole driver searching all directions.

"Aw, shit! Twelve!"

All the action in the back seat stopped, everyone's eyes following the cruiser. When the brake lights came on, Dro smashed the gas pedal, the Mercury tires squealing as the car picked up speed.

"Pull over, nigga! Let me out!" Twenty yelled, opening the door to bail.

"Hold on, nigga! Lemme get to the corner!" Dro said, watching the rearview mirror as he sped down the block.

"Bitch, you bet not tell them shit or I'm comin' to getcho ass! I know where you work!" Tae threatened.

After bending a corner, the Mercury slid to a stop at the curb and the Savages bailed. Dro had just stepped foot on the sidewalk when the police cruiser came fishtailing around the corner. He ran through a yard, throwing the Mac-11 in the bushes before crossing the alley and jumping a seven-foot wooden fence. He dodged kids' toys, sprinting toward the front of the house. The sound of footsteps made him turn to look over his shoulder. The cop who blew through the stop sign was climbing the fence at the back of the yard.

A few steps later, Dro reached the gate at the front of the house. clearing it with a single bounce. Standing six feet tall and 180 pounds, his athleticism and adrenaline made him run faster and jump higher.

Before hitting the ground, he glanced back to check on the cop. Milwaukie's finest got his belt snagged on the gate, hanging him in the air.

Dro continued on, the fear of kidnapping and gun charges keeping his feet moving. He stopped about six blocks later, looking for somewhere to hide. He worried, as unlikely as it seemed, that his description had gone out over the police radio, and he would be caught if he stayed on the street. Plus, the blunts had his chest on fire.

After finding a garage with an abandoned car inside, he climbed in the back seat and curling up on the floor. Parts of T.D. Jakes' message and America's warning played in his mind as he waited. It made him wonder if God was trying to tell him something.

Chapter 2

"Dawg, I swear to God, if you don't shut up," Dro threatened, biting his lip to keep from snapping.

"Nah, nigga. I told you not to leave, and look what happened. What if you'da got locked up? Then what? What was me and Asia s'posed to do?"

"I'm tellin' you, America. Say one more word and I'm giving yo' ass Jay-Z lips."

"Nigga, I wish you would put yo' hands on me. That'll be the last—"

"*Shut the fuck up, bitch!*" Dro yelled , flinching like he was about to hit her.

America jumped, accidentally swerving into oncoming traffic. After righting the car, she gave him an angry look, choosing to remain silent.

During the ride, Dro thought about his get away. He stayed in the garage for two hours before calling America to pick him up. Problem was, he wasn't able to get in touch with his niggas. Tae and Twenty weren't answering their phones. If they got knocked by the fags, there was no telling how much time they would be facing.

After pulling up at home, America started to get out of the car. "You not coming in the house?"

"Nah. Gimme yo' keys. I need to make a move."

"Why don't you take yo' own car? What am I supposed to drive?" she whined.

Dro was tired of all her complaining and bickering. "Nigga, I bought this car. Gimme the mu'fuckin' keys and stop asking so many questions."

"Ugh!" she grunted, slamming the door and throwing the keys at the rear passenger window. The glass broke, sending shards all over the back seat.

Dro took a deep breath, watching as she ran into the house. For a moment he thought about chasing her into the house and catching a domestic violence charge, but he wasn't into hitting women. Plus, his daughter and her cousin were in the house. They didn't need to see that. And he had bigger things to worry about. He needed to find his niggas, so instead of picking a fight, he hopped out of the Camry and kicked out some of the brake lights before walking over to his black Charger.

During the drive, he called Lunatic.

"What it do, Dro?"

"Fuck you been at, nigga? We been trynna call you all morning"

"I'm over here wit' Whisper. We at the condo. What up?"

"Shit all bad, my nigga. You heard from Tae and Twenty?"

"Not since yesterday. What up? Fuck goin' on?"

"I ain't trynna talk about it on the phone. We might be fucked up. I'm on my way. Stay dangerous."

"Savage."

Twenty minutes later Dro pulled up to the East Side Condominiums. After a short elevator ride, he knocked on apartment 15. Prianka answered. Every time he seen the former model from India, he tried not to stare. She was movie-star bad. Fair skin, dark hair, green eyes. She looked like she kicked it with Kardashians.

"Hi, Dro! Whisper and Luna are waiting for you."

He nodded coolly, stepping past her into the plush apartment. Six beautiful ladies wearing sexy nightgowns were lounged around on expensive furniture and mink pillows. The objects of their attention were the men chilling in silk boxers and smoking jackets. Blunts hung from the mouths of Luna and The Ho Whisperer.

"What it do, baby?" the dark-skinned pimp called, lifting a gold jewel-dipped goblet in the air. Whisper was well known around the states and had his hand in a little bit of everything – pimping, escorting, music videos, pornos, and strip clubs.

"What up, playa?" Dro nodded.

Whisper gave him a look. "Watch yo' mouth, youngin'. I'm a pimp, not a playa, playa," he scolded.

"My bad, pimpin'," he apologized before turning to his brother-in-arms. "Luna, what it do, nigga? Lemme holla at you."

Lunatic's personality matched his name. The light-skinned pretty boy was crazy. Got the name when they were younger for shooting a crackhead for always coming short. "What up, nigga? What happened to Tae and Twenty?"

Dro looked at Whisper and the women.

"Speak yo' mind, young Dro," Whisper spoke up after noticing the hesitation. "This like going to Vegas. Everything here stays here."

Lunatic nodded in agreement.

"That move Isaiah put us on went bad. The nigga jaw you broke was Tulip baby daddy."

Lunatic raised an eyebrow. "You mean Isaiah's Tulip?"

"Yeah. And the stupid-ass nigga told her we robbed the niggas. I shot the nigga in his face, but he lived."

Lunatic was heated. "Tell me you bullshitting, my nigga."

"It's real, brah. We kidnapped the bitch this morning. We was trynna find out who the nigga is and knock her   off, but Twelve got on our ass. I think they got the bitch, and

21

maybe Tae and Twenty. I been hittin' them niggas, but they ain't answerin' the phones."

"I'ma kill Isaiah bitch-ass!" Lunatic snapped.

"See, nephew? This is why I was tellin' you that you need to change up yo' hustle," Whisper said, flicking a manicured nail. "Too many headaches, too many hands in the pot, and you facing too much time if you get caught. The best thang goin' will always be pimpin' and hoin'."

"Damn, Dro. She probably tellin' them fags everything. This fucked up, brah," Lunatic stressed.

"Listen, young bloods. It's a dame involved, so I might be able to assist. I ain't neva met a ho that won't go. Put me onto yo' boy, Isaiah, and I'ma give his flower some sunlight. Y'all won't even need guns for this one."

Dro gave the million-dollar pimp a look that said more than words. They were dealing with some serious shit, and he didn't see how a pimp would help. This wasn't a movie, and the look he gave Whisper let him know. Lunatic, on the other hand, seemed to have the weight of the world lifted from his shoulders.

"Okay, Unc. Good lookin'."

"What's up, young Dro? I can tell by the looks you giving that you don't think my money spend. And I respect that, but let me tell you somethin', young Dro. I'm a seasoned vet. Forty years in the streets. I seen my first half-mil when you was in diapers. Judge me after I put in my work. Ya hear me?"

Dro knew he just got checked, but he let the OG have it.

"Ain't nothin' y'all can do but sit back and wait for the other shoe to drop. Lay low and stay off the streets. Y'all can chill for as long as you need, young Dro."

Dro nodded. "Good lookin', 'cause I ain't trynna be out there right now. I threw the Mac, and my fingerprints all over that bitch. They probably raiding my house right now."

"Don't trip, young Dro. Favor for a favor."

The last time the Ho Whisperer spoke those words, it was followed by a robbery that got him ten Gs richer. "You got it."

"I know I got it. I'm the Ho Whisperer, baby boy. Now, I'ma offer you the same thang I did to my nephew. Y'all need to change ya hustles. Shit too hot. If you ever want to get in the managerial field, holla at me. I'll give you the game. For a fee. It's to be sold, not told," he laughed. "Now, roll up something and smoke wit' us. If you wanna take yo' mind off yo' situation, talk to one of my ladies in the other room."

After getting high, Dro took Prianka into the room to get better acquainted. She was currently on her knees, blowing on his tool like it was a musical instrument.

Then his phone rang.

As much as he didn't want to answer, he reached for his pants, hoping it was Tae or Twenty.

"Yeah?"

"Where you at, nigga?" Tae's voice cut through his head.

"Where you at, nigga? I thought you niggas was cooked."

"I'm chillin' at a shorty spot on 49th and Capitol. Come get us. Twenty right here wit' me."

Dro pushed Prianka's head away and reached for his pants. "I'm at Whisper condo wit' Luna. We on our way. Stay dangerous."

"You already know. Savage."

After borrowing one of Whisper's cars, the Savages went to grab their niggas. Lunatic rolled down the block slowly, looking for the address.

"There it is!" Dro said, pointing to a red and white brick house.

Twenty and Tae were watching from the window. As soon as the Buick Regal pulled to the curb, they were walking out of the house. "Damn, that shit was close, nigga!" Twenty grinned climbing into the back seat. "I know you niggas got some gas. Where it at?"

"Stop at the liquor store. I need some Remey," Tae said.

"Fuck, you niggas lose y'all phones?" Dro asked, handing a blunt into the back seat.

"I left that mu'fucka on the dashboard. I didn't even think about it 'til I was trynna hide," Twenty said.

"I dropped my shit while I was runnin'," Tae spoke up. "But you know ain't shit in it, though. That was a throwaway."

"But fuck them phones," Twenty said. "Police got Tulip. If she talkin', we cooked."

"Unc wanna holla at Isaiah about Tulip. I think he might be able to get us out this jam," Lunatic said as he drove.

"Who? Whisper?" Tae asked.

"Yeah. A ho got us into this, and hos his business."

"Nigga, how a million-dollar pimp gon' help us? He ain't got a killa bone in his body," Twenty questioned.

"Unc got connections, nigga. We can't kill er'body. We in some shit if that bitch ran her mouth to the Jakes. We need all the help we can get," Lunatic stressed, defending his uncle.

"He got a point," Dro spoke up. "We gotta play all our cards."

The Savage Life

"Yeah, I hear you niggas, but if I catch that bitch, I'm pushin' her shit back," Twenty said.

"How the fuck that nigga get the name 'The Ho Whisperer'?" Tae asked.

"Y'all remember that show from back in the day with that fine-ass white bitch called The Ghost Whisperer?" Luna asked.

"You talkin' 'bout Jennifer Love Hewitt fine ass," Twenty said.

"Yeah. Unc know the producer. Used to trick on some of his hos back in the day. Unc let him use part of his name to get the show."

The Savages burst out laughing. "Fuck outta here, nigga!" Dro yelled.

"On er'thang I love, fam, Unc plugged."

"But that still don't tell us how he got the name," Twenty said.

"He can talk to hos telepathically. Read they minds and shit. He know if she gon' be a good or bad ho with one conversation."

The Savages laughed again.

"Y'all think I'm bullshittin'? Check this out. Y'all remember that lil'lil' bitch Syraya I was flexin'?"

"Yeah. She was bad. Had you trickin' off in the mall all the time," Tae cracked.

"I wasn't trickin', nigga. I was showing my appreciation. But me and her was beefin' 'bout some petty shit and I holla'ed at Unc about it. Told me to give him the number so he could call her. All she said was hello. Unc told me she wasn't shit. Two months later I found out the bitch was shooting up dog food. A closet dope fiend, my nigga. That's my word."

The Savages burst out laughing again.

J-Blunt

Chapter 3

The Savages spent three days hiding at The Ho Whisperer's condo. While the gunslingers laid low, Whisper had the girls check their houses to see if the police raided.

On the fourth day of no action, the restless jackboys hit the streets again. Dro went to America's house to check on his daughter and drop his baby mama the money to fix her car.

After letting himself into the house, he found America in the kitchen, cooking. "Hey, Dro!" she squealed, giving her baby daddy a hug and kiss, happy he was still free.

"I told you I'ma be good. What you making? Where Asia?"

"The baby with my mom, and I'm making taco casserole. You staying for dinner?"

"Nah. I gotta make a couple moves. How much it cost to fix yo' car?"

"A stack and a half."

He gave her a 'yeah right' look. "Stop playing. A window and back lights don't cost that much."

"But some new shoes do. I seen some Red Bottoms on sale. Don't you want yo' baby mama stepping out on fleek?"

He leaned against the sink, eyeing her from head to toe. She wore a white tank top and black leggings that showed off her thick thighs and phatty. "What I get for all the grip?"

Lust shown in her eyes as she closed the distance between them. "How about you come to my room and let me show you?"

He frowned. "Psh. Yeah right. I get pussy for free. If you call Amy and Shamika over and all four of us get it poppin', that might be worth eight hunnit," he laughed.

America pushed him. "Keep trynna fuck my friends and I'ma fuck you up. Ain't none of they pussy better than mine, anyways."

After a round of sex in the kitchen and giving America the money, Dro grabbed his .40 Glock from the bedroom and left. He stopped to buy some weed before driving to an abandoned house on 29th and Center. After scanning the block for police or signs of suspicious activity, he walked to the side of the house and tapped on the boarded-up windows.

"Crush! Crush!"

A few moments later the back door opened and a skinny, disheveled man walked outside. The dark-skinned man's hair was matted and uncombed, clothes dirty and wrinkled, and he looked like he hadn't showered in weeks.

"Nephew! What's up, baby boy?" he smiled, showing yellow, plaque-stained teeth.

"What up? How you doin', man?"

"I'm okay. You wanna come in and say hi to Trina?"

Dro remembered the last time he went in the house. About twenty crackheads and heroin addicts lived inside amongst piles of garbage. The house smelled like it was filled with dead bodies. "Nah, I'm good. I don't got that much time. Come take a walk with me to the gas station. You hungry?"

The junkie licked his dry and chapped lips. "I sho is, nephew. You came right on time."

Dro looked him over as they walked. Crush's shoes were dirty and curled up at the toes, clothes wrinkled. "What happened to the clothes I gave you? Why you rockin' this dirty shit? And when was the last time you took a shower?"

"You know I don't need much of nothing. Long as I got clothes on my back and somewhere to lay my head, I'm good. I gave some of the stuff to my friends. They needed it.

They don't got family to come check up on 'em. We got to look out for each other out here. We stick together in that house."

"C'mon, Crush. I gave that to you, man. I can't take care of all them. Why don't you go to rehab and get back with Candice?"

"Hey! I already told you we not to go there!" he snapped.

"My bad, Unc. I'm just trynna look out for you."

"And you do. I'm okay. How are your mother and sisters?"

"I haven't been to the house in about a week, but I talk to Shanice and Kailah almost every day. They good. Getting big. I got some pictures on my phone if you wanna see."

"Nah, nah. Seeing the girls might break me down. I just wanted to know how they were doing. What about Marcia?"

"Moms is good. Her and Lenny still going strong."

"Lenny don't deserve her, you know that? He won't ever replace yo' pops. He was her soul mate. Ask her. I know she a Christian now, but I knew her when she wasn't, and man, she really loved yo' daddy. Only reason she with Lenny was because my gun jammed. If I woulda had a revolver, Robert would still be here. But I gotta live with that. I accept that I got my little brother killed. That's why I'm out here like this, nephew. This my punishment."

"You didn't get him killed, Crush. Wasn't nothing you could do, man. I'm my father's son, so I know what the stick-up life is like. Being out here in the streets ain't yo' karma. This yo' choice. You say the word and I'll put you in a house and take you shopping. You just gotta leave that diesel alone."

"This my vice, nephew. I ever tell you about Sisyphus, the evil king of Corinth from Greek mythology? For his cruel deed, Karma sentenced him to eternal torture in Hades when he died. His punishment was rolling a big rock uphill. As soon as he got to the top, he lost his strength and the rock would roll back down the hill. He did this every day, all day for eternity. I'm Sisyphus, nephew. I tried to get off these streets. Every time I feel like I shook the dope or drinking, I wake up the next day hungover from drinking and broke from a dope binge. This my big rock. I graduated college, served in the military, worked all kinds of jobs, but look at me now."

"It's still yo' choice, Unc. Whenever you say you ready, I got you."

"Yeah, I hear you. I don't know what I would do without you. So, what's up with you? How the stick-up life treating you?"

"I had a crazy couple of days. Made a move about a week ago, then found out the nigga that put us on the move told his girl. Turned out he had us rob her baby daddy. We tried to catch the girl and get rid of her, but got sweated by the police. They got her now, and I think she told 'em er'thang."

"Damn, nephew. It sounds like you might be in some shit. Don't you think you should leave town?"

"I was layin' low for a couple days. Nothing came up, so I'ma head home and chill. Stay out the way for a lil'lil' while."

"You ever thought about what you gon' do when you can't rob people no more? Sun won't shine forever."

"Nah, not really. Life moves so fast in the streets that I live it day-by-day. I told myself I would quit when I got a hunnit Gs, but most of the time I spend the money as soon as I get it."

"Today should be a lesson for you, nephew. If you don't come up with a plan, you've already planned to fail. Living life in the fast lane will get you two things: a cell or casket. This last robbery sounds like you gettin' chased by both. The only other option is to get out while you can. Come up with a plan. You smart. Street smart and book smart. Getting locked up and reading was a blessing in disguise. You know more than the average street nigga. You have potential. Don't waste it like me and your father did."

After buying his uncle something to eat and giving him his last hundred dollars, Dro headed home. He had been driving for ten minutes when he noticed a police cruiser a couple cars back. He didn't know if they were onto him, so he kept calm, watching the mirror intently.

At the next Intersection he turned, panicking a little when the police car followed. Tulip's face popped into his head. If she told the police they kidnapped her, he was facing at least forty years. He pulled the Glock onto his lap, watching the cops in the rearview. He couldn't tell if they were running his plates.

Then the sirens flashed. *Whoop-whoop!*

"Bitch-ass shit!" Dro cursed.

He wasn't sure what they were pulling him over for or how many charges they would put on him. Robbery, murder, kidnapping. Dying in a cell wasn't an option. He also didn't want to be the latest poster man for the Black Lives Matter movement, so he pocketed the Glock, pulled to the side of the road, and parked.

The officers got out their car, one on the driver's side, the other on the passenger side. When they were almost at his window, Dro slammed the car into gear and smashed the gas. The sports car shot through the intersection, dodging traffic.

He watched the mirror as the police ran to their car. Knowing he couldn't outrun their car or radio, he turned onto

31

a side street. Halfway down the block, he bailed, leaving the keys in the ignition. The car was registered in America's name, and she knew the drill. Somebody stole it.

The tires on the police cruiser screeched around the corner as he booked it through a yard. After tossing the pistol and zig-zagging a couple of blocks, he slowed, the blunts making his chest burn.

Four blocks away he pulled out his phone and called Twenty.

"Young Dro! What it do?"

"I need you to come get me! Them fags just—"

"Dro, what up, nigga?" Twenty called when Dro stopped talking.

Two police had come through the yard a few houses ahead of him. When they began running toward him, he spun and ran in the opposite direction. That's when a police car fishtailed around the corner. He turned to break through a yard when the police giving chase pulled their guns.

"Get on the ground, now, or I'll blow your fucking head off!" one of them yelled.

As much as he didn't want to go to jail, he also didn't want to get killed. And it wasn't until he got on his knees that he remembered the half ounce of weed in his pocket.

Chapter 4

Dro hated jail. The off-white paint on the walls, the way the floors shined, and especially the smell. Like depression, fear, and stress. He had spent countless seconds, minutes, and hours behind bars and knew the inside of a cell very well.

The interrogation room made him nervous. He was cuffed to the wall, awaiting the interrogators. They found the weed, pistol, and suspected him of fleeing and eluding in the Charger.

But none of those charges concerned him. What had his life flashing before his eyes was Tulip. Hundreds of years in prison jumped around in his head like kids in a bounce house. His girls jumped around with them. Asia and America would be devastated if he didn't come home. The thought of his daughter growing up without him was soul crushing.

Noise at the door got his attention. A short, light-skinned nigga with brushed waves walked in. He wore a gold chain, iced-out medallion, and designer clothes. If they weren't in a police station, Dro would've taken him to be a street nigga.

"'Sup, homie?" he nodded, placing a cell phone on the table.

Dro remained cool. "You tell me."

"A'ight, brah. I'm Detective Scott. You being held on gun and drug charges. You wanna make a statement?"

Dro knew the rules. Shut the fuck up. You have the right to remain silent. If you don't say shit, they won't know shit. "Nah, I'm good. I don't got nothing to say."

The detective gave him a long, searching look. "Listen, my nigga. I'ma keep it a hunnit with you. We know that was yo' banger. It's in the lab right now being dusted for prints. You and I know yo' prints is on it. Do us both a favor and make a statement."

Dro laughed, shaking his head.

"You think this a game. huh? Okay. If I gotta jump through hoops, shit gon' be worse. All you got is a weak-ass possession of dope on yo' record from a couple years ago. Did a year up north. Ain't really shit. I tell you what. Cop to the pistol and I'ma give you a ticket for the weed. Plus, I'll forget about the fleeing and eluding."

Dro thought about the wannabe street nigga's spiel and had to admit the copper had a mouth piece. He had tricked many idiots into telling on themselves. But Dro wasn't one of those idiots, and the most valuable lesson he learned up north was to keep his mouth shut. Plus, he didn't mention Tulip. As far as Dro was concerned, the police didn't have shit on him.

"I'm good on that statement. I told you I don't got nothin' to say. I want a lawyer. Make sure you turn on yo' phone and record that."

Detective Scott became frustrated. "Listen, my nigga, gettin' a lawyer only gon' make this worse. Just gimme a statement about the pistol, and when you get arraigned, I'ma personally tell the court commissioner how you cooperated. That probably get you probation."

Dro laughed at his antics. "I'm good, brah. Let me get that lawyer."

"A'ight. If that's how you want it. Cool," he said, getting up and walking toward the door. "I was trynna help anotha nigga stay out them white folks' systems, but if you wanna go back up north, cool." After opening the door, he paused to take one more look at Dro. "You sure you want to do this? Once I leave, I'm gone."

Dro nodded confidently. "Lawyer."

When the detective left, a uniform stepped into the room, un-cuffing him and leading him to a holding cell. During the walk, he led Dro down a hall filled with interrogation rooms. From behind the closed doors there was crying, screaming, and hushed whispers from people copping deals.

After a short walk, he was locked in another cell. As soon as his ass hit the concrete slab, he began to pray. He had done a lot of praying since being arrested. Being locked in a cage for the rest of his life was terrifying. And even though he was guilty of the crimes he was being questioned for, he still prayed to God for another chance at freedom.

Eventually he prayed himself to sleep.

Keys at the door jarred him awake. A female officer stepped into the cell. "You Ruben Patrick?"

"Yeah."

"Come with me."

"Where we going?"

"Boss told me to get your pic and prints."

Dro's heart sank. "Then what?"

"I think you going to booking."

After getting his prints and picture taken, Dro was locked back in the holding cell. He prayed some more before considering the possibilities. A misdemeanor for the weed. Ten years for the pistol. Five more for fleeing and eluding. He would get bail tomorrow, maybe the next day. In the long run, he would probably end up back in prison for a couple years since he was already a felon. Crush's words about getting out of the street played heavily in his mind.

An hour later, the female officer was back. "C'mon, Patrick. Time to go home."

Figuring she was calling jail his new home brought on a bout of depression, but something made him ask, "You mean *home*-home?"

She laughed. "Yeah. The detectives told me to let you go and give you a ticket for possession."

The smile on his face told of the joy filling his soul. For a moment he thought about grabbing the officer and kissing her, but instead of getting in more trouble for some kind of sexual assault, he allowed the police officer to lead him toward the door.

After signing the ticket, he was given his only property item – a cell phone – and released. It was a little past two in the morning and he was broke, but he didn't care. He was free.

He powered on the phone and tried to call America. A low battery sign flashed on the screen and the phone cut off. "What the fuck?" he cursed, trying to turn on the phone again. "Fuck," he breathed when it cut off again.

He took a moment to consider his next move as he stood outside the police station. He thought about going back in and asking to make a phone call, but reconsidered. It would be just his luck that the police connected him to another crime as soon as he walked back in. So, he got to stepping.

Street lights flashed yellow and red as he walked through a deserted intersection. The city was asleep. The only people on the streets were the police, dope fiends, hustlers, hos, and jackboys. Since he was familiar with the area, he headed for a gas station a couple blocks away, planning to use the phone.

He was half a block from the gas station when he seen a female on the other side of the street with a monster booty. She had the kind of ass that demanded attention, and he was going to use her phone and get her number.

There were a few cars coming toward him, but he ignored them, stepping into the street. "Ay, shorty! Lemme holla –"

A horn blaring and tires screeching made him lose sight of Ms. Monster Booty. He turned just in time to see an SUV skidding toward him. He couldn't move fast enough, and the collision sent him flying into the air and rolling a few feet.

"Oh my God! Oh my God! Are you okay?" a woman screamed, jumping out of the truck and running over.

The adrenalin didn't allow him to feel the pain right away, so he jumped to his feet, ready to snap. When he seen the woman that ran him over, every derogatory name he wanted to call her vanished from his mind. The only word that remained was *fine*. The woman was the epitome of beautiful, hair set in a naturally curly afro that showed her mixed heritage, perfectly arched eyebrows, a small nose, full lips and dimples in both cheeks, perfect teeth. Skin the color of beach sand, and her body was banging. She had the kind of curves women got surgery to imitate. She looked so good that even though Dro was fucked up, he still wanted to shoot his shot.

"Yeah. I'm good," he managed, dusting himself off and checking the burns and scratches on his arms.

"I'm so sorry, sir. I didn't see you. I swear!" she apologized.

"You need to watch where you goin'."

"I'm sorry. Do you need me to call you an ambulance? Do you want me to take you to the hospital?"

He got macho. "Nah, I'm good. Ain't nothin' broke. I don't like the police or doctors. I'm straight."

"At least let me give you a ride. Where are you going?"

"I'm on my way home."

"You're not a stalker or serial killer, are you?" she asked, making an attempt at humor as they climbed into her truck.

"Nah. But if I was, you'd be in trouble."

A gospel song by Mary Mary played softly from the speakers, and the truck smelled like perfume.

"Where to?" she asked after they closed the doors.

He thought about going to America's house, but figured the argument about the car, him being hurt, and the woman dropping him off wasn't worth it. "60th and Locust."

"You sure are far from home."

"Yeah. Something came up."

"That's a pretty good neighborhood. Who do you know there?" He thought he heard a little suspicion in her voice.

"I live there."

"I don't gotta worry about any crazy baby's mothers, do I? I don't want any drama," she laughed, half joking.

"That wasn't funny. I live by myself. And I don't got baby mamas. I got one daughter, and she lives with her mother," he said matter-of-factly.

"Sorry," she apologized. "I didn't mean to upset you."

"Yep," he nodded, deciding he didn't like her. Although she was beautiful, the uppity attitude made her ugly. As far as he was concerned, they didn't have anything else to talk about, so they rode in silence.

"My name is Forever. You are?"

He glanced at her and seen curiosity in her pretty brown eyes. She was trying to be nice. And after all, he was in her truck. "I'm Dro."

She scoffed, mouth hanging open, brows furrowing. "I'm sorry, did you say 'Dro'? Like, hydro weed?"

"Yeah. Dro. What with you, shorty? You from the boonies or something?"

"No. I'm sorry, I just never had a real street person in my truck with a ghetto name."

"A ghetto name, huh?" He chuckled, shaking his head and biting his tongue to keep from giving her the business.

"Oh my God. I did it again. I'm sorry, Hydro. I didn't mean it like that."

He laughed again, waving her off. There was no need to respond. It would only make things worse.

"Listen, man. I don't know how to talk to you or what to say, and I'm sorry. I'm not even from Wisconsin. I'm from a little town in North Dakota called Grand Forks. I don't know anything about the hood. I graduated from college, go to church, and go to work. If I say the wrong things, I don't mean to. It's just I've never had an actual conversation with somebody like... you," she winced.

Dro thought about what she said. It made sense. "So, that explains your choice of words. Okay, Forever. My name is Ruben. Nice to meet you," he said, extending a hand.

She breathed a sigh of relief as they shook. "Nice to meet you, Ruben."

"I wish I could say the same, but considering you ran me over, I can't."

"I'm really sorry about that."

"I know. I should've been watching where I was going. You have a unique name. How did you get it?"

She shifted in her seat a little. "Honestly, I don't know."

"How you don't know how you got your name? What did your parents say?"

"Hey, could we talk about something different? No offense, but I don't know you well enough to talk about my family."

The hot and cold was becoming too much, but for the sake of being a good dude, he respected her request. "Okay. So, what is a college-educated, church-going, working girl doing out here so late, running people over?"

"Oh, Lord! Don't even get me started," she laughed. "But to make a long story short, a girl from church was having boyfriend problems and called me. Helping her lasted all night. I was kind of praying and talking to God when I hit you. Closed my eyes for one second and there you were."

"Blaming God for this one, huh? That's a first," he laughed.

"I wasn't blaming God. It's really your fault for not looking both ways before crossing the street. So, what are you doing out so late?"

He considered lying to her. She was a prima donna and would turn up her nose at the truth. But he also didn't want to lie. "Just got out of jail. They gave me a ticket for weed."

Her body went stiff, face flat. " Oh. Okay."

He noticed her reaction. "What does that mean? 'Okay' what?"

"Nothing. I didn't say anything."

"It ain't what you said, but what you didn't say, and how you reacted. I ain't no dope fiend or drug dealer, but I smoke weed. You should know about that since you went to college. Plus, recreational and medicinal marijuana is legal in a lot of states. And it's safer than opioids."

"I'm not looking to argue with you, Ruben. It's fine. It's your life. I can't tell you how to live."

He knew she wanted to say more, but had another uppity negro attack, and he let her have it. They were a few blocks from his house, and he was tired of her many moods.

"Which house?" she asked after turning onto his block.

"White and blue one. Couple houses down. Bushes out front."

She was impressed. "Wow. Nice house."

He didn't respond. When she pulled to the curb, he reached for the door, a sharp pain shooting though his body. "Shh! Ah."

"Do you need help?"

He waved her off. "Nah, I got it," he mumbled, struggling to get out of the truck. Stiffness had set in during the ride, and the entire right side of his body was on fire.

"Are you sure you don't want me to take you to the hospital?"

He limped from the truck in serious pain, refusing to give her the satisfaction of seeing him look weak. "Nope. I got it."

She watched him for a couple moments, and right when she was about to drive away, he got her attention.

"Hey, Forever!"

"Yeah? Do you want to go to the hospital?"

"Nah. Judge not that ye not be judged. For what judgment you judge, you will be judged; and with what measure you use, it will be measured back to you."

The mug she gave him before driving away gave him temporary relief from the aches and pains. It felt good, knocking her from the high horse she rode.

The satisfaction was short-lived when he bent down to find the spare key hidden in the bed of rocks surrounding the bushes. After struggling to stand again, he opened the door and limped around to find the phone charger before walking into the bathroom. After plugging in his phone and leaving it on the sink, he ran a bath. After stripping naked, he checked his body for damage. A giant bruise covered his right leg from hip to shin. Scratches covered his arms.

The hot water eased some of the pain, putting him to sleep. He was awakened by the ringing phone. I was America. "Why the police calling me, talking about somebody jumping out of yo' car? Why you didn't call and let me know, nigga? Got the police coming to my house, waking me up and shit."

He hung up the phone and turned it off, having enough arguing for one night. After drying off, he limped to bed and fell right to sleep.

A couple hours later he was awakened by aches and pains. After powering on the phone, he checked the time. 8:47 AM. After checking messages, he called Twenty.

"What's good, nigga? Fuck happened yesterday?"

He let out a short, audible breath as he recapped one of the worst days he'd had in a long time. "My night was all fucked up. I tried to call you because I was runnin' from the police. They took me down and popped me for some weed. Tried to put my .40 on me, but couldn't. They didn't say nothin' about Tulip. I think she kept her mouth closed. Either that or they didn't know who I was. Then, on top of that, after they let me go, I got ran over. My shit all fucked up, and I'm sore as fuck."

"Damn, my nigga. All that shit sound fucked up. You might need a vacation or retire."

"Shit, I thought about it."

"And I can't believe that bitch held her water. But that don't mean she didn't give us up to her baby daddy. Oh, and you ain't gon' believe this, but that nigga Isaiah dead."

"For real?"

"Yeah. They found that nigga in the garbage can wit' five to the dome."

"Damn. Did y'all –"

"Nope. We think Tulip nigga did that shit. Lunatic said his name, remember?"

Dro felt no sympathy. "That's what his bitch-ass get. Nigga shouldn't've told the bitch shit."

"Yeah. I'm on that same shit. So, you good? You don't think they gon' charge you wit' nothin' else?"

"I don't know. But I need some Percs or somethin' for this pain. What you got?"

"I got a plug for you. You at the crib?"

"Yeah. I'm chillin' all day. My shit fucked up."

"I got you, my nigga. I'ma ride down in a minute. Stay dangerous."

"Savage."

J-Blunt

Chapter 5

"No, Daddy! That's not how you do it!" Asia complained, throwing a tantrum while her father checked her Facebook page. "Them all my friends from school."

"Watch out, lil'lil' one. I know what I'm doing. Making sure you safe on here. It's a lot of crazy people out here, and I ain't playin' that shit. Yo' momma shouldn't even let you have a Facebook page. You too young," Dro lectured.

"No, I'm not. A lot of kids be on Facebook. You just old."

He cut his eyes at his daughter. "Old? Baby, I'm twenty-five. Ain't even hit my prime yet. All yo' friends' mommas stay in my lane."

"That's because they old, too!" she laughed.

"Keep talking shit and we gon' watch the movie I wanna watch. I still ain't seen Avengers: Endgame yet."

"You know I love you, Daddy," she smiled, walking over to hug him. "I'm sorry."

"I thought so. Just let me finish checking something, and then we can leave."

"C'mon, Daddy! You gon' make us late," she whined, tugging his arm, trying to pull him up from the couch.

"Okay. Five more minutes."

"Daddy! Ugh!" she grunted, rolling her eyes.

"Keep doing that and yo' eyes gon' get stuck in the back of yo' head." When he was satisfied that everything was cool on Asia's social media, he did a quick search of his own.

When her picture popped onto the screen, there was a tingle in his stomach. A little more than a week had passed since his run-in with Forever. She was the finest woman he had ever seen, and a part of him wished they had met under different circumstances so he could've gotten to know her.

45

Then he remembered the look she gave him after he quoted the scripture. Like she wanted to kill him. But the look wasn't enough to stop him from wanting to be her friend. She was too bad not to make one more attempt, So he sent her a friend request before taking Asia to the movies.

After watching The Secret Life of Pets 2, he dropped his daughter off at home and drove toward Tae's house. He was stopped at the gas station when he got a notification on his phone. Forever had accepted his friend request.

Not wanting to waste a moment, he sent her a message, quoting Ecclesiastes 3:1. *To everything there is a season, a time for every purpose under Heaven.*

She responded with Psalms 1:1. *Blessed are they who don't walk in the counsel of the ungodly, nor stand in the path of sinners.*

He laughed before typing another message. *Let's FaceTime.*

Why?

So you can see my leg.

When her face popped onto the screen, Dro had to give her a compliment. "Damn. You are pretty."

She smiled. "Hi, Ruben. Thank you."

"I take it you made it home without running over nobody else?"

"Ha ha," she laughed sarcastically. "How is your leg?"

"You broke it."

She looked horrified. "Oh my God! I'm so sorry, Ruben."

He burst out laughing.

"What's funny? Why are you laughing?"

"Because the look on yo' face was priceless."

Anger flashed in her eyes when she realized she was the butt of a joke. "You know what? You're a real jerk."

"My bad. But my leg is good. Couple scars and bruises."

"Well, that's good to hear. And again, sorry for running you over."

"It's all good. And you know how you can make it up to me?"

She frowned. "What are you talking about?"

"By agreeing to be my friend. Not just on Facebook."

Her eyes squinted really small. "Why? So you can have your baby mothers and thots stalking me?"

He burst out laughing. "Wait. Say 'thots' again. That was too funny."

"See, that's why we can't be friends. You're always making fun of me."

"Okay. I'm sorry. But if you woulda heard the way you said 'thots', you woulda laughed, too. So, can we be friends?"

"No. I don't got time for drama, or to be stalked by thots."

The playfulness vanished from his features. "You know what? For a Christian, you quick to judge a nigga. Oh yeah, I forgot. That's what y'all do. Think y'all better than everybody. What makes you think I got a bunch of girls chasing me? You putting labels on me before getting to know me. I told you I got one daughter and one baby mama. And I live alone. In a good neighborhood. Quit thinkin' everybody that ain't saved is a liar."

She looked like she wanted to tell him off, but remained quiet. And then she blinked away the irritation. "I'm sorry, Ruben. I was wrong for that. But we can't be friends."

"That's how it is, huh? A nigga come correct and y'all still be trippin'?" he hissed, hoping to draw her into a debate.

47

"What are you talking about, y'all?" she sassed. "Don't be lumping me in with those low-class women you deal with."

"I don't deal with low-class women. I got standards. And you just like all the rest of them nose-high-in-the-air-types. Judging me by appearance. That don't mean I ain't a good dude. I take care of my shorty. We just came back from the movies. And I got good credit. Pay all my bills on time. You a trip. Still judging."

"So, you can read minds now? You know what I think about you? And this is not even about you. This is about what I want."

"What is it about then?"

She let out a frustrated breath. "I don't want to argue. Just trust me, Ruben. You don't want to be my friend."

"So, you read minds, too?"

She shook her head, letting out a chuckle. "You are being way too persistent."

"Only way to break resistance."

"Why do you want to be my friend? I judge too much, right?"

"Yeah. You real judgmental. But I'm a sinner, and I might end up back in jail and need another ride home. I might also need some prayer, because the pain in my legs is making me smoke more weed. Being friends will make us even."

She shook her head again. "Will you ever get past me running you over?"

"I only forgive my friends."

"Okay, Ruben. But don't be calling me all times of the night. I work. And only call when you need help. Like prayer or advice."

He smiled. "Deal."

***

"My nigga!" Tae yelled when Dro walked in the house. The cornrow-wearing gunslinger lived alone in a single family house on 29th and Villard. The Savages were meeting to discuss their next move.

"'Sup with you, niggas?" Dro asked, plopping down on the couch.

"Waiting on you so we can holla 'bout how we gon' get the paper," Luna said, rubbing his palms together.

"Fuck you was at, anyway?" Tae asked.

"I had to take my baby girl on a date to the movies. Gotta be a daddy, too, nigga."

"Ol' Daddy of the Year-ass nigga!" Twenty laughed.

"Hell yeah! I love my baby girl," Dro said proudly. "But what the move is? Let's talk about gettin' this bag."

Twenty got serious. "We talkin' a hunnit Gs. Maybe a couple bricks."

Dro's eyes lit up. "On what?"

"Yeah, boy!" Lunatic yelled, giving his best Flavor Flav impersonation.

"Who the vic?" Dro asked.

"Vics," Tae clarified.

Dro raised an eyebrow. "How many niggas we talkin' 'bout?"

"Nigga, how many moves I done put us on? If I say it's a green light, we move."

"What that gotta do with anything? I just wanted to know how many niggas might be in the house."

"'Cause it seem like you questioning my move, nigga. I been plotting this for a minute. Got this shit down to a science. I know er'thang 'bout these niggas. I know –"

"How many niggas in the house?" Dro cut him off.

Some kind of hostility flashed in Tae's eyes. "Three or four. If you woulda listened to the rest of what I was about to say, I was gon' get to it."

"What up wit' you, Tae? You feeling some type of way, brah?" Dro asked.

"You is trippin' a lil'lil' bit," Lunatic cut in.

Tae paused for a moment, catching himself. "My bad, Dro. Shit been crazy wit' my mama and brothers. Shit got me ready to get on one."

"I don't give a fuck how many niggas in that house. For a hunnit racks, I'm in that bitch," Twenty grinned.

"And it's one of Monster spots, too," Tae added.

Dro forgot about the little skirmish with Tae, eyes growing wide as full moons. "Ooh, shit! I been wanting to get in that nigga pockets for a minute."

Monster was the man in Milwaukee, more popular in the hood than the mayor and aldermen. Everybody knew who was at the top of the food chain on the north side. The streets said he got work from a Mexican cartel a hundred bricks at a time. And everybody who crossed him was either dead or run out of town.

"We gon' touch them pockets in a few days. This Sunday, when it ain't a lot of traffic and them niggas sleeping or hung over from clubbing the night before," Tae promised.

"So, how we goin' in? How y'all wanna play it?"

Tae threw him a duffle bag. There were clothes inside. "Fuck is this?" Dro asked.

"Look at it, nigga," Tae breathed, vexed by all the questions.

Dro unfolded a navy blue t-shirt. POLICE was written across the front in big, block yellow letters. Also in the bag were police badges hanging from silver chains and police hats.

"Oh, hell yeah!" Dro smiled. "This it, right here!"

Twenty took credit. "Thank me for this one."

"Oh, yeah. I meant to tell y'all that Whisper found Tulip," Lunatic said, switching gears.

All the Savages gave him sideways looks. "How long you knew this?" Twenty asked.

"I knew since this morning. I forgot to say something earlier. She part of the stable now."

Tae pulled the .44 Magnum from under the couch pillow. "Let's go get that bitch."

"Nah. Unc got her. She on the team. Her baby daddy is a nigga named J-Mac. He from The City. Said he went home to get some of his niggas and they lookin' for us. Her, too. She think he gon' knock her ass off," Lunatic explained.

Twenty checked the extended clip on the .380. "I don't give a fuck who team she on. That bitch gotta go."

Lunatic didn't want to make the call to his uncle, but the Savages had made their decision. No one would stop them from getting to Tulip, not even The Ho Whisperer. "I told my niggas about the flower. They want her gone."

"C'mon, nephew. Calm yo' hyenas down. She got promise. I can't let this one go to waste."

Lunatic looked around at his niggas' faces as they listened to the call on speaker. The Savages gave stone, uncompromising stares.

"Nah, Unc. She gotta go. She know too much."

"Damn, nephew!" the pimp lamented. "Okay. When I send her out, I'ma text you. You muthafuckas owe me for this one."

***

Turning tricks wasn't Tulip's thing. She hadn't done it since she was a teenager in the hood trying to get a new pair of shoes. But Whisper promised protection from the Savages and J-Mac. Her baby daddy swore to kill her when he found out Isaiah had set him up. Tulip had nowhere to hide. When the pimp showed up out of nowhere promising protection, she took the offer, knowing she needed help from someone with real power in the streets.

After parking her Ford Focus, she peered up at the house through the darkness, searching for signs of life inside. There was a light on in the living room. After one last check of her make-up in the mirror, she reached for the door handle.

Twenty sat in the car parked across the street, watching his victim. When she climbed from the car, so did he.

Terror shown in her eyes when she recognized his face, but it was too late to scream or run. The .380 sparked seven times, all of the bullets aiming for her chest and face.

She died before she hit the ground.

Chapter 6

Dro used the key to let himself into America's house. Figuring everybody was asleep, he went right to the bedroom, ready to pass out.

When he walked into the room, the first thing he noticed was the candles.

"I was wondering when you was gon' show up," America purred, slapping a naked thigh. The 24-year-old vixen was sprawled on the bed in a sexy pose, wearing French-cut lingerie. A butterfly vibrator and dildo were in arm's reach. Tank crooned about rough sex from the speakers.

"I woulda came soon if you let me know about all this," he said, licking his lips and eyeing her half-naked body. His baby was strapped and sexy as hell. Big titties, small waist, wide hips, and thick thighs that hugged him just right when he was deep in them guts.

"If I called, it wouldn't be a surprise," she smiled, crawling toward him on her hands and knees. "Now, stop talking and get naked, nigga."

Dro's pants and boxers dropped to his ankles like bricks were in the pockets. His dick stood out like a missile. "You know I stay ready. King shit!"

"Come here, king."

When he walked to the edge of the bed, America opened her mouth and slid his dick inside. Her hands found his balls and began massaging. She gave head game like a champ. America chewed on him like she was making love with her mouth.

"Oh shit, baby!" Dro moaned, lost in the zone, loving the blow job. Then she rolled on her back, head hanging off the bed, and let him fuck her mouth until he busted down her throat.

After drinking her medicine, she sat up in bed, opening her legs. "Come give me mine, nigga."

"Let me see that pussy, baby!" Dro grinned, reaching down and snatching off her panties.

America's pussy was beautiful, Brazilian waxed with no hair or razor bumps, and fat lips slick with juice. Dro dove between her shit like he had a knife and fork, sliding two fingers in her pussy while sucking her clit.

"Oh yeah, baby! Get it, nigga! Get it!" she cheered, grabbing the back of his head.

He kept sucking and fingering her until she came, wetting his lips with her cum. Then he grabbed the vibrator. "Get on them knees."

America assumed the position – face down, ass up. "You know how I like it, baby. Put that butterfly on my pussy and fuck me in the ass."

***

Dro woke up the next morning in bed alone. America had gone to her retail job at a local boutique, and Asia was in school. After taking a moment to collect his thoughts, he reached for the weed in his pants pocket and rolled a blunt. He checked the phone as he smoked, deciding none of the missed calls and texts needed to be returned right away.

Then Forever popped into his head. It had been a couple days since they talked, and he wanted to see her, so he hit her up.

"I thought I said only call in emergencies. This better be important," she said seriously.

Dro smiled when he seen her. She was super bad and wore light make-up, her hair combed into a bushy ponytail. "It is. I missed you."

She squinted until her eyes were barely visible, face stern. "Ruben, I'm at work. I have to meet with a family in about fifteen minutes. What do you want?"

"Chill out. I thought we was friends. I was just calling to say 'what up'. I didn't know you was at work."

"Where else would I be on Tuesday at ten in the morning? Why aren't you at work? Do you have a job?"

He thought fast, on his toes. "Yeah. I took the day off. My leg, you know?"

She finally smiled. "You are something else, man. I'm not apologizing anymore."

"You don't have to. We friends now, right? What kind of work do you do?"

"I'm a social worker. Why?"

"What time do you get off?"

"Why? I don't want you keeping tabs on me."

"Did you eat lunch?"

"This is personal. I thought we were prayer friends only?"

"Stop playing. I just want to know if you ate lunch. Where the harm in that?"

"Actually, I'm working through lunch. Told you, I have an important meeting."

"Let me take you to dinner when you get off work."

She frowned. "What? No. I'm not going on a date with you."

"I'm not asking you to go on a date. Unless you wanna go on a date. I just wanted to know if I could buy you dinner. You said you working through lunch."

"I don't know," she hesitated.

"You need to think about if you hungry or not?"

"So, you're a comedian, too?"

"Nah. I just wanna know why you gotta think about getting something to eat after work."

"It's not that, Ruben. I just don't do the dating thing."

"I thought we agreed it wasn't a date."

She thought for a moment. "You really want to take me out to eat? You want to buy me dinner?"

"Yeah. That's it. No funny business."

"Okay. I get off at 5:00. I'll be at your place around 5:30."

***

Dro stepped in front of the mirror, checking himself over while listening to T.D. Jakes preach in the background. Lining was crisp. Brushed waves looked like an ocean. Face clean shaven except for a perfectly-trimmed mustache. His peanut butter complexion shone like new money from a coat of Shea butter face moisturizer. He wore a blue sweater vest, white button-up underneath, beige slacks, and loafers. A rose gold Rolex cuffed on his wrist demanded attention.

The time read 5:26.

Four minutes later, the doorbell rang. Forever stood on the stoop, looking perfect. She wore a flowery blouse, teal flare-bottomed pants, and heels. The 18-inch gold chain with a small crucifix was the perfect accessory.

"What up? I see you stay fly," Dro commented.

She looked him over from head to toe. "No, no. You're the one that's fly. You can really dress it up. Looks like you're going on a date."

"Work hard, play hard," he grinned. "You want to come in real quick while I grab my phone and lock up?"

When he walked toward the back of the house, Forever took a look around. She expected the house to look like a mix between college kid and bachelor pad, but was pleasantly surprised at how neat and kept it was. Hardwood floors shined, and a nice, black three-piece sofa set matched the drapes. A flat screen TV hung on the wall, paused on the screen was a prominent black preacher from a Super Church.

"You ready?" Dro asked, grabbing the remote to cut off the TV.

"Was this for me?" she asked, pointing to the screen.

Dro looked confused. "What? My TV?"

"No. You watching T.D. Jakes. Are you trying to impress me?"

He lit out a laugh. "Is that how low you think of me? Think I'll use God to help make a good first impression?"

After realizing her mistake, she backtracked. "I'm sorry. I didn't mean it like that. I just didn't know you were into watching church DVDs."

"Lot you don't know about me. Got a whole rack of videos next to my Xbox. I know you didn't miss those," he pointed.

She swallowed her pride. "You got me, okay? I was judging, and I'm sorry. So, did you have any place in mind to eat?"

They ended up at a soul food restaurant downtown. Sammy's served the best grilled lemon chicken in Milwaukee.

"When you said your name was Dro and you just got out of jail, I pegged you for a thug. I'm sorry. Do you go to church?"

"Nah, I don't go to church. Think I might light on fire if I go in one. But I always had a thing for listening to good preachers since I was young. Grew up in church. Mom and step-pops Holy Ghost filled. Took me and my sisters to church events all week long."

"Oh, you have siblings? How old are they?"

"Two lil'lil' sisters. Shanice is seventeen, Kailah is fourteen."

"So, what have you done so bad that you can't go to church?"

Dro thought on how to answer the question and deciding not to answer at all. "When I was ten, one of the craziest things happened to me. A preacher prophesized over me and told me I had a calling in my life to do amazing things in the Kingdom of God."

Her eyes grew wide, threatening to pop out of her skull. "Oh my God, Ruben! That is incredible."

"I didn't think so when I was young. Had me spooked."

"I'm so amazed. Do you want to come to church with me tomorrow? Our preacher is really good. The choir, too."

Dro almost choked on his delicious lemon chicken. He had to take a sip of wine.

"You okay?" Forever asked.

"Yeah, I'm good. Something got caught in my throat."

"Well, will you come to church with me?"

"C'mon, Forever. I haven't been to church in ten years."

"That doesn't matter. Everybody in church is not saved. You wouldn't believe some of the things I seen church people do. Don't even get me started."

"But I'm worse than all of them."

"So was Paul. He used to kill Christians, but went on to write most of the books in the New Testament."

He laughed. "How about we switch subjects? I don't think I'm ready to go to church."

"Okay. So, what do you think about the weather?"

He laughed again. "We about to have a conversation about weather? For real?"

"You wanted to switch subjects."

"How about we talk about you? Do you have anybody important in your life?"

"Sounds like you're asking if I have a boyfriend. If I did, I wouldn't be here with you. I don't really know anybody or have a social life. I've only been here for a year, and I haven't dated in years. Not really a serial dater or relationship kind of girl. This is the most I've talked to a man that wasn't a coworker or church friend in years."

"Not a relationship kinda girl? What do you do to pass time?"

"I'm too focused on God and my clients to be thinking about a man. Plus, y'all lie too much."

"That brush you painting with got a pretty wide stroke."

She rolled her neck from side to side. "That's because I have a big canvas."

He eyed her for a moment. "You ever been in a serious relationship?"

She looked away. "Yeah. Once. Big mistake."

"What happened?"

"He lied to me."

"So, he is indicting all men?"

"No. You guys indict yourselves. Men are scandalous."

"And women ain't?"

She peered at him. "Do you lie, Ruben?"

"Sometimes. Yeah. Who don't?"

"How old are you? What do you do for a living?"

He frowned. "I didn't know you took a criminal justice course on interrogation in college."

"I just want to know more about you."

"I'm 25, and I work in repo."

"Repoing what? Can all your coworkers afford a Rolex?"

"This was a gift. And I take whatever needs to be took."

"What's that supposed to mean?"

"Exactly what I said."

"I don't believe you. Not driving a brand new Charger and living in your neighborhood. Or wearing that watch. Where did you really get it?"

He laughed. "I repoed it."

"Do you sell drugs?"

"Nope."

"Run scams?"

"C'mon, Forever."

"Are you a pimp?"

He mugged her. "Hell nah!"

"Are you a bank robber? Tell me what you do, because I know you're not a repo man."

He let out a long breath, unable to hide his frustration. "Listen, Forever. I'm not a dope boy, con man, pimp, or none of the other stuff you said. I'm not lying about working in repo, and I'm not your ex. Now, can we enjoy the food? Your chicken is getting cold."

She relaxed a little, taking off some of the edge. "I'm sorry, Ruben. I told you I don't get out much. You think I'm crazy, don't you?"

He tried not to laugh, but couldn't hold back. "A little, yeah. But it's okay. At least you ain't girl-from-the-hood crazy. They shoot you and set your car on fire. You didn't burn up yo' ex's car, did you?"

"No," she laughed. "But I thought about it."

After sharing another laugh, he asked the question that had been on his tongue for the past half hour. "I liked getting to know you, even though you got a lil'lil' bit of detective in you. I wanna take you out again. On a real date."

"Whoa, Ruben! Slow down. I don't know about all that," she smiled, taking a sip from the glass of white wine.

"So, it's like that? Wanna run up a hundred-dollar tab and flake out on me? Normally if I took a girl out to eat, I'd be hittin' that later on."

She burst out laughing, spitting wine all over the table, food, and Ruben.

"Damn, girl!" he flinched.

"Oh my God! I'm so sorry!" she apologized, trying to wipe the table with napkins.

"Now I'm definitely seeing you again," Ruben mumbled, wiping wine from his sweater vest. "Done spit wine all over my clothes."

"I'll make a deal with you, Ruben. If you come to church with me tomorrow, I'll go to dinner with you. On a real date."

He sat back in the chair and thought for a moment. He had something important to do tomorrow, but he also wanted to see her again. "What time does the service start?"

"Eight o'clock."

J-Blunt

Chapter 7

"What the hell am I doing?" Dro questioned aloud as he parked behind Forever's Buick truck. In a couple of hours, he would meet with the Savages to rob somebody. He felt like the devil. Somehow he knew God would punish him for this.

The people who walked toward the church dressed in their Sunday best looked immune to sin, as if temptation bounced off them like water did duck feathers. He considered driving away, knowing he didn't belong in their midst, but his mother and Lenny raised him to be a man of his word.

The Holy Cathedral was a huge brick building with a tall steeple atop. He stepped through the wooden double doors, hoping the black suit and Steve Maddens didn't catch fire.

After breathing a sigh of relief for not bursting into flames, he began looking for his girl. She wasn't hard to find. Nobody in the church could shine in her light. Not even Jesus. And the white dress made her look like a fine-ass angel.

"Hi, Ruben! I'm glad you made it," she smiled, giving him a hug.

"Only if you knew," he laughed nervously. "I thought about driving away twice. Thought I was gon' burn up when I walked in here."

"You're crazy!" she laughed. "C'mon so we can get a good seat."

The service kicked off with a bang. First Lady McClain started with scripture reading and a fiery prayer that got the church rocking. The choir followed, singing four songs that stirred the congregation some more. Then the preacher came to deliver the word. Pastor McClain was short and stocky with light brown skin. When he opened his mouth to preach, Dro's skin began tingling.

"Glory, hallelujah! Glory be to God!"

The church echoed his praise, lifting their voices to worship God.

"Last night, while I was in my prayer closet, the Lord spoke to me. He told me to check myself before I wreck myself. And I came to deliver that word to the church. Check yourself before you wreck yourself."

Everyone in the church laughed except Ruben.

***

"So, what did you think about the service?" Forever asked after they stepped outside.

"Like he was talking to me. I can't stop thinking about some of the stuff he said. The life God put us in is larger than the life we're living. If we continue to ignore God, He will remove the hedge of protection and the devil will have his way. Pastor McClain need to record some sermons. Got me thinking about changing my life."

"Well, maybe that's what you needed to hear. You said God has a calling on you. Maybe he was trying to tell you something."

"Forever!" a short, brown-skinned woman called, walking over.

"Oh Lord!" Forever cried. "I hope she don't need my help again."

"Do unto others as you want done to you," Dro laughed.

"Last time she needed my help, I ran you over."

His smile vanished. "Man, I hope she don't need yo' help."

"Hey, girl. How are you?" the woman asked, exchanging hugs.

"I'm good, Sasha. Blessed. How are you?"

"I'm feeling good. Made some changes in my life," she said before turning to Dro. "Who is he? Have you been here before?"

"I'm Ruben," he smiled, extending a hand. "This is my first time coming here."

"Hey, Ruben. Don't be a stranger," she smiled, giving Forever a wink.

"We're just friends," she clarified.

"Friends that look like him get me in trouble," she flirted.

Forever rolled her eyes. "Leave him alone. What did you want?"

Sasha hesitated. "Um, I was wondering if you could help me with something."

Dro took his cue. "Forever, I got something to do. Can I call you later for some prayer?"

"Better not be after nine o'clock."

***

"Damn, nigga! Where you at?" Twenty complained.

"I'm on my way right now. I just left the house."

"Fuck you been? We been callin' you for, like, thirty minutes."

"I had some shit to take care of," he said, not wanting to tell his niggas about Forever or going to church.

"A'ight, nigga. Hurry up. Stay dangerous."

"Savage."

He got to Tae's house ten minutes later. After changing into the police gear and locking the church clothes in the trunk, he went in the house.

"'Bout time, nigga!" Lunatic breathed.

"Fuck you was at? You know we agreed on ten o'clock," Tae fussed.

"You niggas chill. I know Twenty just told y'all what I said. I had my phone off this morning. Now, let's go get this money."

Tae and Dro had a brief staredown before they left the house, piling into an unmarked maroon sedan with tinted windows. The ride to the drug house was silent, all the jackers on point. Focused. Ready. When they pulled onto the block, the first thing they noticed were the cars. A blue Audi, a black Benz, and a candy-apple green old school on big rims.

"A'ight. Y'all niggas know the move," Tae spoke up. "If these niggas flex, bust they shit open. Stay dangerous."

"Savage," they echoed.

The hitters piled out of the car, armed to the teeth. Tae had an AP nine with a 32-shot clip. Lunatic carried a black 12-gauge pump with an infrared beam. Dro and Twenty had Glock .40s with thirty-round extensions.

After running up on the porch, Dro and Lunatic counted to three before kicking the door in. Tae and Twenty took off into the house. "Freeze! Police! Nobody move!"

The four men in the living room froze when they seen the uniforms and guns, hands flying in the air.

"How many in here?" Lunatic asked, pointing the shotgun in a fat, black nigga's face.

"Just us."

"All of y'all get on the floor. Keep yo' hands where we can see 'em," Twenty ordered.

The men moved quickly, dropping onto their stomachs, arms outstretched.

"Where the dope and the money, nigga?" Lunatic asked a tall, skinny nigga with long braids.

"At cho bitch house, nigga," he mugged.

Lunatic looked amused, cocking the shotgun, clearing the chamber and sending a round flying across the room. Then he flipped the gun around, holding the barrel like an axe handle as he brought the stock down on the man's head. "Where the dope at, bitch-ass nigga? Where the dope? Where the fuck is the dope?" he asked over and over as he beat the man unconscious.

"In the kitchen!" the fat, black nigga screamed. "Top cabinet, in the cereal boxes."

"Look in the cereal boxes!" Twenty called.

Tae came back in the living room holding a gold AK-47 and a bag of money. "Look what I found," he said, eyeing the gun like it was a woman.

"That bitch pretty!" Twenty whistled.

Dro came into the living room, smiling and holding a box of cereal. Inside was nine ounces of heroin. "I got the work!"

"A'ight, y'all. We gon' let y'all go," Lunatic said. "Don't got time to do the paperwork. What do y'all say?"

"Fuck you, nigga. We know y'all ain't the police," a light-skinned nigga with long, permed hair and manicured nails spat.

Lunatic moved toward him with the shotgun.

"I got it," Twenty grinned, pulling a lighter from his pocket. He bent over the slick talker and struck the lighter. The man's perm caught fire like he had an accelerant in his hair. He jumped up, screaming and patting his head, leaving a trail of smoke while trying to put out the fire.

The Savages ran out of the house, busting up with laughter. They were piling into the car when Tae began screaming, "Watch out, fam!"

The fat, black nigga ran onto the porch, firing a nine mil.
Pop-pop-pop-pop-pop-pop!
Tae flipped up the AK-47 and fired back.
Tat-tat-tat-tat-tat-tat-tat-tat!
"Ah, shit!" Dro yelled, falling into the car. "I'm hit! I'm hit!"

The fat, black nigga ran from the chopper bullets, and the Savages piled into the car.

"Where you hit at?" Lunatic asked, searching Dro's body as Twenty sped away.

"In the back of my leg! Ah, shit!" Dro cursed, Pastor McClain's words playing in his mind.

Tae knelt over the back seat and tied a shirt around the leg wound. "How many times you get hit?"

"Just once, I think," Dro winced.

"How bad is it?" Twenty asked, whipping the sedan through traffic.

"It's bad." Lunatic answered. "Nigga bleeding all over the seat. We gotta get 'im to the hospital."

"Ay, take that police shit off," Tae said, pulling the police gear from Dro's body.

"You know the move, nigga," Twenty said. "You was on the other side of town. Tell 'em you got robbed and shot. I'ma drop you off at the emergency room door."

"I know how that shit go!" Dro yelled. "Just get me to the mu'fuckin' hospital!"

Chapter 8

Dro couldn't believe he was in jail again. And this time it wasn't looking good. Pastor McClain's sermon echoed in his head on repeat, the volume turned up loud. As he sat in the wheelchair, handcuffed to the wall inside the interrogation room, he wondered if God had dropped the hedge of protection around him. The devil seemed to be having his way.

When the door opened, Dro's mind was taken off Lucifer and brought back to the moment.

"Small muthafuckin' world, ain't it?" Detective Scott smiled as he walked into the room. "How is that wheelchair treating you?" the cop/thug asked.

"'Sup, lil'lil' nigga?" his partner, Detective Jackson asked, sucking the back of his teeth.

Instead of giving them a reaction, Dro remained silent. This was the third interrogation in two days. He knew the drill.

"Look at the lil'lil' nigga trynna be tough," Jackson smirked.

"What's good, Ruben? Last time I seen you, I had a good deal for you. Cop to the heat and get probation. You come back a couple weeks later shot up. What's goin' on, fam?" Scott asked, setting a 12-inch tablet on the table.

The electronic device grabbed Dro's attention. Somehow he knew that whatever was on the electronic device would give them a leg up.

Then the cops pulled up chairs on either side of him, blocking him in the middle. "Tell me how you got shot again before I show you how we know you lyin'," Jackson said.

"I told y'all, I got robbed."

The detectives laughed. "Right. By the two white boys on 50th and Silver Spring," Scott smiled.

"Yeah."

"Okay. The car that dropped you off at the hospital, did it look like this?" Jackson asked, tapping the tablet screen. Footage from a security camera it front of the hospital showed the unmarked car pull up to the emergency room exit. Dro limped from, the car before it pulled away.

"Well, was that the car?" Jackson asked again.

Dro invoked his fifth amendment right and remained silent.

Detective Scott nudged his arm, leaning close. "Ruben, c'mon, man. Say something. You see the problem we got, right? Nah? Well, check this out. The car that dropped you off at the hospital was used in a robbery on 33rd and Walnut. And this is gon' blow yo' mind, my nigga. Apparently, the police was in this car. Did you see 'em?"

Silence.

"You look sick, lil'lil' nigga!" Jackson laughed, pulling out a pack of cigarettes. "Wanna Newport?"

"Where the rest of yo' clothes, man? I wanna see how real that shit looked. Did y'all even have badges?" Scott asked.

"Robbing Monster's spot dressed up like the police woulda been smart had y'all dumbasses checked them for guns," Jackson chuckled.

"When do I get my phone call? I need to call my lawyer," Dro spoke up, tired of their shit. On the outside he remained calm, but on the inside he panicked. They had him in a jam, knew the whole move. It was only a matter of time before they nailed him to the cross.

"Oh, so you can talk," Jackson laughed. "For a minute I thought yo' ass went mute."

"Yeah, I can talk. And I want my mu'fuckin' phone call. I been here for more than 24 hours, and I still ain't got my call. Y'all violating my mu'fuckin' rights!"

"Oh, shit. Lil'Lil' nigga know his rights," Scott laughed.

"A'ight, Ruben. We'll get you that phone call," Jackson said. "But I got one more question. When we catch them other niggas that was with you, which one of y'all is going to testify first?"

***

Dro sat in the wheelchair inside the holding cell, steaming with anger and frightened for his freedom. The detectives had clowned him. They knew everything, and they still hadn't given him a phone call. They left him in the holding cell to stew, using all the tactics to get him to tell on himself, but Dro wouldn't fold. He couldn't. Thoughts of Asia growing up without him was all the motivation he needed to keep his mouth closed.

"Patrick!" a man called from the other side of the door. When it opened, a white cop stepped into the room. "Your lawyer is here."·

Behind the cop was a clean-cut, brown-skinned man wearing a tailored blue suit. "Officer, I need a moment with my client."

The cop stepped out and closed the door.

"Mr. Patrick, I'm your attorney, Brandon Williams," he introduced, extending a hand. "I got a call from some of your friends that you might need my help. How are you holding up?"

Dro let out a long breath. "Good, now that you here."

"How long have you been here?"

"About a day and a half."

"Were your rights violated? Did you confess to anything?"

"They didn't give me a phone call. And I didn't confess to shit. I got robbed and shot. Some people driving past seen it and gave me a ride to the hospital. Now they trynna say I robbed somebody."

He nodded. "That lines up with everything I've been told. They're questioning you about a shootout that happened on Walnut. There are no victims, only a witness or two that said the police were shooting at someone in the house. The detectives are saying they didn't have anyone in the area and the car that dropped you off was involved in the shooting."

"I told 'em I didn't know nothing about that."

"Okay. Give me a few minutes and I'll see if I can get you out of here. Hold tight."

Relief washed over Dro when the lawyer left the room. Monster's boys didn't snitch or call the police. It must've been a nosey neighbor, he reasoned. They didn't have anything on him. They had been holding him to see if he would tell on himself.

Fifteen minutes later Brandon came back smiling. "I spoke with the detectives and the captain. They don't have anything solid, but they do have witnesses and want you to do a line-up. I urged them to do it within the hour."

Dro's heart felt like it was about to explode. "A line-up? For what? I wasn't there."

"They have probable cause. Witnesses say they seen the car that dropped you off at the scene of a shooting."

"C'mon, Brandon. I'ma probably be the only one in a wheelchair in the line-up. They trynna set me up," Dro argued.

"I won't let them do that to you. I'll be in there, too. Can't let them coerce the witnesses."

It took less than an hour for the detectives to assemble the lineup. None of the men resembled Dro in the slightest way. One of them was six-foot-five and dark-skinned with cornrows. Another was short and light-skinned. He also had cornrows. The last one looked albino, and he also had braids. The only thing they had in common with Dro was being black and locked up. He was the only one in a wheelchair. Didn't take a genius to figure out he was in a shoot-out.

"Number three, yell, 'Watch out, fam!'" the detective ordered from behind the two-way mirror.

The tall nigga did what he was told.

"Number two, repeat that," the detective said.

As the second man spoke the words, Dro realized the people in the lineup resembled Tae and Luna. And just when he was starting to feel good, his number was called.

"Number one, say the same line."

"Watch out, fam!" Dro yelled, sounding like a mix between Michael Jackson and Prince. The niggas in the lineup thought he was being funny, but he didn't care. He was trying to stay out of jail.

The lineup was over as quick as it started, and Dro was wheeled back into the holding cell. He sat in the wheelchair, fidgeting nervously like he was sitting on pins and needles.

Twenty minutes later, the cell door was unlocked and Brandon walked in wearing a poker face. Dro's heart triple-timed as he awaited the news.

"You ready to go?" he smiled.

Dro's eyes grew wide. "Seriously? We good?"

"Yep. Witnesses picked out the second guy with braids. Said he had a machine gun."

Dro sank back in the chair, emotionally drained, relief flooding his body. "Let's get the fuck outta here."

"Do you need a ride?"

***

"My nigga!" Twenty yelled, sounding high as a kite.

"Where you at, fam? One of y'all gotta come get me. Y'all ain't gon' believe this shit," Dro said, hopping around the house, looking for some plastic to wrap his leg so he could take a shower.

"I see they let cho ass out. Did you see the lawyer we sent? That was Whisper guy. We called the hospital and found out Twelve snatched you and got on that ASAP."

"That shit was right on time, too. Them bitches ain't wanna gimme my call. I thought a nigga was cooked. They knew the whole move. I don't wanna say too much on the phone. One of y'all come and get me. My Charger still by Tae house."

"A'ight, my nigga. I'm on my way. Stay dangerous."

"You know it. Savage."

After hanging up, Dro found some plastic bags under the kitchen sink and taped them around his leg before getting in the shower. As the water sprayed his body, he thought about all the close calls he had as of late. Twice the police had him in a jam. He could've been easily facing hundreds of years in prison. Somehow he managed to escape unscathed. He wondered how many chances he had left.

***

"So. is they finna hit you wit' charges?" Twenty asked, weaving the Chrysler 300 through traffic.

Dro took a pull from the blunt of loud. "I don't think so. They picked out a nigga that looked like Tae. Whoever them witnesses is, they heard him tell us to watch out. Had us screaming it out during the line-up."

"Damn. That's fucked up. What if they come lookin' for fam?"

Dro thought for a moment. "Ain't shit we can do but let 'im know. Play it by ear and lay low for a lil'lil' while. But what you niggas do with that car? They got the footage from the hospital and seen y'all drop me off. My DNA all over that back seat."

"Stop playin'. You know we on top of that. Set that bitch on fire and made sure it burned all the way up. They ain't findin' shit on us. Crackers got you spooked, huh?" Twenty laughed.

"I ain't trynna do anotha bid, my nigga. I been in two jams and managed to get out. I don't know how many chances I got left."

"Those the risks of the game, my nigga. Either that or a grave. And I'd rather be judged by twelve than carried by six."

"You ever thought about quittin' this shit and gettin' on some square shit?"

Twenty glanced over, eyebrows wrinkled. "And do what? This all I know. I ain't got no diplomas. I didn't even graduate high school. Neva had a job. This it for me. Either I hit licks or starve. And I ain't goin' hungry. I'll neva be broke long as I can take a nigga shit."

Dro didn't agree with Twenty's outlook. He had a daughter and wanted more out of life. Problem was, he didn't know what. But he couldn't tell Twenty that. The dreadlock-wearing, pistol-carrying goon was too street to understand a nigga not wanting to be in the streets anymore. "Yeah. I hear you, fam."

When they pulled up to Tae's house, the elder Savage was waiting on the porch. After hopping in the back seat, he threw a paper bag on Dro's lap. "You good, nigga?"

"Yeah. Didn't hit no arteries. What's in here?" he asked, looking in the bag.

"Yo' cut. Fifteen Gs. You should gimme some of that back a take a couple ounces of this dog food. You niggas trynna leave me to sell all the dope. Know I don't hustle."

"Shit, neither do I. You the one wit' dope boys in yo' family. You can get it off. What we hit them niggas for, anyway?"

"Fifty Gs and nine zips that you niggas leavin' me and Lunatic to flip.

"Hold on, nigga! Don't you owe me some more money?"

"Hell nah! Unless you wanna sell the work yo'self."

"Fuck that shit. I'm cool. I was just tellin' Twenty that they pulled a nigga out the line-up that looked like you. The witnesses seen you shooting that chopper."

Tae smiled. "Oh yeah? That's what's up. How much they know?"

"They know we hit them niggas and had a shoot-out. Seen y'all drop me off at the hospital. The car was tinted, so they didn't see nobody faces. As long as that car gone, we good."

"Yeah, we burned that bitch up. But fuck it if they did have somethin' on me. I'ma be fresh as hell if the feds watchin'. Tell them bitches to come get me."

"A'ight. I ain't trynna make the news, so I'ma get little. Gotta pick up this damn prescription," Dro said, getting out and limping toward his Charger. "You niggas stay dangerous."

"You know it. Savage."

Chapter 9

"Damn, Unc! You clean up nice. Looking and smelling like new money," Dro commented when Crush walked out of the bathroom.

"Been a minute since I had a shower and some new clothes. Good lookin' out, nephew."

"I paid up the room for a week. That way you can get a break from all those people in the house. Here go some pocket change, too."

Crush pocketed the $200. "Thanks, nephew. Boy, I don't know what I would do without you."

"You know I got you, Unc. C'mon. Let's hit the barber shop and get you crispy and grab something to eat."

After leaving the hotel, they hopped in Dro's Charger, heading to the barbershop. "So, what's goin' on with your leg?" Crush asked.

"Got shot. Streets got me on crutches. America had me locked in the house, trynna baby me for the last couple days. I had to get the fuck outta there."

"Yeah, that's the thang with the streets. Chris Brown might as well had been talking about the streets when he said 'these hos ain't loyal'," Crush laughed. "So, what happened?"

"Hit one of Monster spots. We ran in dressed like the police. Had a shoot-out on the way out."

Crush looked surprised. "Damn, nephew. That was bold."

"We wanted to get in and out without shooting, but that didn't work."

"But it was creative. What you tell them after you got shot?"

"That I got robbed and shot by some white boys on Silver Spring. But they knew better. Got the video from the emergency room camera showing Twenty an' 'em drop me off. Luckily we had tints on the windows, 'cause they knew what happened. Somebody called the police and told them about the shoot-out. I had to do a line-up and everything. They picked out a nigga that looked like Tae."

"Man, that was another close call, nephew. I don't know how you keep on slipping out of they grasp like that. If you was a cat, I bet you used up most of those nine lives. Whatever happened with the girl y'all kidnapped? They didn't say nothing about that?"

"Nah. We took care of that. And I don't know how I keep getting out of these jams. I been thinking about it a lot. It be seeming like God be trynna tell me shit. The crazy thing is, before we hit Monster's house, I went to church. The preacher said –"

"You went to church before you robbed somebody?" Crush asked, looking at Dro like he was crazy.

"I had to. It was a prior engagement that I couldn't shake."

"Boy, you can't be playin' with God like that."

"I know, Unc. You know I was brought up in church. I know what the book say. The last thing I wanna do is play with God. But it's this girl, man. Forever."

Crush smiled knowingly, getting lost in reverie. Flashes of happiness, joy, and good times passing across his face. "It's always about a woman. Forever, huh? Is she anything like Asia's mother?"

"Nah. America from the hood. Forever from North Dakota. They night and day. Forever is focused on her career, loves her job as a social worker, likes to help kids.

And she's a Christian. And celibate. Play hard to get, but I know she feeling me."

Crush laughed. "Sounds like she outta yo' league, nephew."

"C'mon, Unc. I'm valid on every level. God ain't made a woman outta my league."

"I'm just playing with you, man. She sounds like a catch. Does she know what you do in the streets?"

"Nah. I told her I'm a repo man."

Crush laughed again. "Well, it ain't really a lie. You do take from people. But if she is everything you say, you gon' have to tell her the truth. And the truth about that is, she probably won't accept it."

Dro didn't respond. Deep inside, he knew Crush was right.

That's why he lied to her about his occupation. She was a square. No way she wanted to be around a stick-up kid.

"The one thing you have in your favor is that opposites attract. Some kind of universal law or something. Good is always drawn to bad like darkness is drawn to light."

Dro gave his uncle a look. "Damn, Crush. That was good shit. You write poetry?"

"There's a lot you don't know about me, son. I used to be a beast back in my day. Another thing is, since she took you to church, it sounds like she wants to bring the best out of you. That's a good quality to have in somebody that loves you. To have somebody in your corner that believes in you more than you believe in yourself is rare. It's God sent. Reminds me of the Bible, where they talk about the virtuous woman. Her price is far above rubies. She will do her husband good and no evil. I used to know a woman like that."

Dro looked over and seen Crush struggling to hold his composure. "You talking about Aunty Candice, huh?"

Crush ignored the question, asking one of his own. "Dro, you ever give some more thought to getting out of the streets?"

"Not really, but getting shot and going to jail opened my eyes to a lot of shit. I know I can't do this forever. My daughter needs me. Shit, I need me. I just don't know what else to do. I been taking niggas' shit for a long time, and I feel like I'm good at it."

Crush laughed. "Apparently not that good. You got shot and been in jail twice in the last month. You on they radar now, nephew."

Dro thought about Detectives Scott and Jackson. "Yeah, I know. They want me, too."

"What if Forever is your way out, nephew? What if she's your guardian angel?"

Dro gave his uncle's words some thought. "When good things fall into your lap, you gotta leave all the bullshit behind. Forget everything that you know and lose everything you want so you can keep what you need."

***

After kicking it with his uncle, Dro decided to hit the hood and see what was cracking. During the drive, he replayed several pieces of the conversation with his uncle. The old man was right. He needed to find a way out. Getting shot and going to jail was a sign of things to come. Bad things. Things he didn't want.

Fifteen minutes later he pulled up to a gray house in the middle of the block on 42nd and Garfield. Most of the murders that happened in Milwaukee were around this north side neighborhood. Even in daylight, nobody was safe. No matter the weather – rain, sleet, or snow – being on Garfield was like being in Iraq. Niggas suffered from post traumatic stress disorders like war vets, except they didn't go to expensive doctors. They treated their illness with drugs and alcohol.

"What up, nigga?" Nu-Nu grinned. The big, light-skinned man was a regular on the block. He stayed posted up like he was a stop sign.

"What it do, nigga?" Dro asked, grabbing his crutches and limping onto the sidewalk.

"Niggas heard about that move y'all pulled the other day."

Dro gave him a look. "Fuck you talkin' 'bout, nigga?"

"I'm talkin' 'bout how you got that slug in yo' leg. We heard y'all went in as them people. Had a detective car and er'thang."

"Damn, nigga! What, you Channel 6 News or somethin'? How you find out about that shit?"

"You know Luna can't hold water. Came through here selling ounces of diesel for the low."

"That nigga a trip." Dro shook his head before climbing up on the porch to show the niggas on the block love. Trouble, Rich Boy, Demarco, and Fresh sat on the porch smoking blunts. "'Sup wit' chu niggas?"

"We hittin' the highway in a couple hours," Rich Boy said. "Got some hos in Chicago that want real niggas!"

That got Dro's attention. "For real? Where you meet 'em at?"

"On the book. You know a nigga stay lookin' for somethin' new to slide in. All the hos love squeezin' the teddy bear," Rich Boy laughed, grabbing a handful of stomach.

"Count me in. I need to get outta town for a couple days. What time we leaving?"

"Soon as Swoop get here," Trouble spoke up. "He supposed to be on his way."

Dro pulled out his phone and began texting America to let her know he was going out of town. He was about to put the phone in his pocket when it rang. A smile as wide as the Equator played on his face when the name popped on the screen.

"I knew you would call. Ready to admit how much you like my company?"

"Wow, Ruben. Humility is really your thing, huh?" Forever laughed.

"I try. But what's up with you? What you on?"

"I'm okay. Haven't heard from you in a couple days. You never called me for prayer, and I just wanted to see how you were doing."

"So, you checking up on me now? What, you worried I might get run over again?"

"See, this is why we can't be friends. You don't know how to let things go. Bye, Ruben."

"Wait, wait, wait! You know I'm just playing. And my bad for not calling. I've had a crazy couple days."

"It's okay. I know how busy repo men can be," she said sarcastically.

"Right. Right. But how have you been?" he asked, switching to her. "Catch me up on what yo' week been like."

"I'm okay. Trying to enjoy every single day that my boss is on vacation. I'm pretty sure he hates me."

"Hate is a strong word. Maybe you intimidate him. Lotta dudes intimidated by strong women."

"No, I'm pretty sure he hates me. He asked me on a date awhile back and I turned him down. He doesn't handle rejection well. Been giving me a hard time ever since."

"Oh. Damn. Yeah, he might hate you. But speaking of dates, when will you honor our dinner date? I went to church."

"How does this Sunday sound? Around eight o'clock," she laughed.

"How do a few days earlier sound? Without preachers and choirs?" Dro countered.

"Um. What are you doing now?"

He looked down at his leg. It needed a couple more days before he could ditch the crutches. "Nothing, really. Just kicking it with some of my boys."

"Well, how about you leave your friends and take me to get something to eat?"

The trip to Chicago was cancelled. "Tell me where you live. I'm on my way."

J-Blunt

Chapter 10

After leaving the hood, Dro went to his storage unit and traded the Charger for his candy-red Z06 Corvette on 22-inch chrome wheels. He knew grabbing the car might be a bad idea. Forever was inquisitive, but his desire to flex outweighed common sense.

After stopping at the grocery store to pick up a few things, he headed over to her apartment in the suburbs of West Allis. When he found her door on the second floor, he knocked.

"Hi, Ruben," she smiled brightly. After noticing the crutches, she frowned. "What happened to your leg? Are you okay?"

"Yeah. I'm good. Work accident. Can I come in?"

"Yeah. Sure," she said before stepping aside. "What happened?"

"Got hit by a car," he joked.

She gave him a look like she was scolding a child. "Stop playing. What happened, seriously?"

"I tried to take somebody's car, and they let me know how much they didn't like it and ran me over."

Her eyes grew wide. "Are you serious?"

"Yeah. The company has all their information. The police looking into it. Ain't nothing bad. I should be done with these crutches in a couple days."

She poked out her bottom lip. "Aw, poor baby. You sure you want to go out? We can reschedule if you want."

He looked her over from head to toe, loving the way the purple dress hugged her curves. "Nah, I can't let you waste that dress. Plus, I'm already here."

She gave him a searching look. "Are you sure? This is an old dress. I've had it for years."

"Well, you make it look new. And I'm good. Ready?"

"Okay. Let me grab my purse. Thanks for the compliment."

Dro watched her perfect booty cheeks jiggle as she walked to the back of the apartment. While she grabbed her belongings, he looked around. She had a gray-and-yellow theme. She also had some African art and sculptures, but what caught his eye was the picture of Forever. She looked to be about six or seven years old, wore a pink tutu, white tights, and had her hair in pigtails. She was also missing a front tooth. He picked up the picture and began laughing.

"What are you laughing at?" she asked, appearing from the bedroom.

"You."

She snatched the picture and sat it back on the table. "Don' be laughing at me. That's my favorite picture. First dance recital. If you're done laughing, I'm ready."

When they walked outside, she looked around for his Charger. "Where are you parked?"

He pointed to the Corvette. "Right there."

She stopped in her tracks, eyes wide with surprise. "What do you do, Ruben? I know you're not a repo man."

He limped over to open the passenger door, smiling. "I'm a repo man. For real. Get in. I have a surprise."

She crossed her arms over her chest, continuing to stare at him.

"Chill, Forever. This car is ten years old. I bought it at an auction. I can't afford this car off the lot. Now, are you coming?"

After a little more staring, she got in the car. "I don't believe you. I hope you're not lying to me, Ruben."

"I'ma take this as a sign you like my car. Thanks."

During the ride, conversation flowed smoothly. Thirty minutes later he pulled into the parking lot of Bradford Beach.

"What are we doing here?" Forever asked. "I thought we were going to dinner."

"This where we eating at. I told you it was a surprise."

She looked around. "This is the beach. Unless they built a restaurant in Lake Michigan that I can't see, where is the food?"

"Relax, Forever. I got everything we need. Trust me."

She smiled, liking that he had everything under control. "Okay. You lead, I follow."

"That's what I'm talking about. Push that button and pop the trunk for me." After limping to the back of the car, he grabbed his crutches from the trunk and handed Forever the picnic basket and white sheet that was next to the sub woofers.

"Oh, good one, Ruben! I've never been on a picnic."

Hi smiled confidently. "I told you, I got you."

After finding a spot on the beach, they ate club sandwiches, mixed fruit bowls, and had cheesecake for dessert. When they had their fill, they lay back drinking champagne they had smuggled in and looking out over the lake.

"Wow, Ruben. This is amazing. I can't remember the last time I felt so relaxed and comfortable."

"I was thinking the same thing," he said, letting out a satisfied sigh. "Tell me about you. You know a lot about me, and I barely know you."

"What do you want to know?"

"About your family. Your upbringing. How did you end up in Milwaukee?"

She was quiet for a moment, staring at a sailboat. "I was raised in foster homes."

He couldn't hide the surprised look. "Seriously?"

"Yep. I never got to meet my parents. Or family. I've lived with nine different foster families. I don't have a real family."

"Damn. I don't even know what to say. Have you ever tried to find yo' parents?"

A single tear rolled down her face. "I've thought about it. Guess I never got the courage to start the process. I didn't want to spend all the time and energy looking for them and have them reject me. After all, they gave me up. They obviously didn't want me. What am I supposed to say? 'Hey, Mom. Hey, Dad. Here's the baby you gave up twenty-eight years ago.'" The single tear that rolled down her face transformed into a rushing river. Then she got angry. "I mean, how do you just leave your baby? Just give her to strangers and never look back? How can you bring a child into this world and not care if she lives or dies? How do people do that?"

Dro remained silent. He didn't have answers for her questions and didn't want to say the wrong thing.

"I'm sorry, Ruben. This was a beautiful date, but I need to leave. Can you take me home?" she asked, standing.

"Whoa! Wait," he said, standing too quickly and hurting his leg. "Ah, shit! Wait, Forever. It's okay."

"No, it's not. I want to leave. Take me home."

He reached out and touched her arm. "Hey, chill. It's okay. We don't have to talk about your family no more."

"I just want to leave, Ruben. Please."

"Okay. We gone," he said, reaching for his crutches. They cleaned up the remnants of their picnic on the beach and walked silently to the Corvette. The drive was also silent, a first.

"God don't put more on us than we can bear," Dro said. Forever didn't respond, so he continued. "I heard a preacher say that God can take our mess and turn it into a message. I believe that. I'm a mess, but I think one day, whenever I give up my will, God will use me. And if he can use me, shit, he can use anybody. What don't kill you makes you stronger. I think you're a strong woman. You'll be okay."

The words covered her body like a warm blanket, touching her soul. "Thank you," she mumbled.

"Can I ask you a question?"

"Yeah."

"Will you tell me some more about your upbringing?"

She mugged him. "Didn't you just see what I went through?"

"Just hear me out. I ain't no psychologist or nothing, but I heard that it's best to talk about the stuff we keep inside. We have to get it out so it doesn't poison us. It's part of that 'the truth will set you free' stuff."

Forever though about what he said, surprised he actually cared. He wasn't judging and wanted to listen to her issues. This man from the other side of the tracks, whom she would have never given a chance, was trying to help. "Can you stop and get something to drink? Something strong."

After stopping at a liquor store, Dro limped inside and bought a bottle of Patron. When he gave it to Forever, she attacked the bottle. And when the liquor began to take effect, she relived her past.

"I bounced around from foster home to foster home for as long as r could remember. I always got molested by my foster brothers, and when I told an adult, they blamed me and sent me to another family. When I was twelve, I finally landed with the perfect family. I had two little sisters I was crazy about. And even though the family was white, they accepted my light skin like I was flesh and blood. Then puberty came, and I wasn't the only one that noticed."

She became quiet, drinking more of the Patron. Dro remained patient, driving around aimlessly while she found the courage to tell her story.

"I was fourteen the first time he touched me. I fell asleep on the couch and thought I was dreaming when I felt a hand go up my shirt. When I opened my eyes, my foster father was kneeling next to me with a horny look on his face. Scared the hell out of me, and I ran to my room and locked the door. Laid awake all night. I looked at Mr. Morton like he was my dad. He was supposed to love and protect me. I was confused for a long time after he touched me. I wanted to tell my foster mom, but I was scared of being sent to a group home or another family. Plus, I loved my little sisters and wanted a real family. So, I stayed quiet. And the more my body developed, the more aggressive he got. When I told him I would tell his wife, he threatened to kill me. When I was sixteen, he raped me. That's how I lost my virginity."

"Damn," Ruben mumbled.

"He raped me a couple more times before we were caught in the act by his wife. She called the police and he got sent to prison for ten years, and I got sent to a group home."

"They shoulda killed his bitch-ass," Dro mugged.

"Do you think I'm crazy?"

Dro took his eyes off the road for a moment. "Are you serious? Why would I think that? I'm not gon' judge you for being taken advantage of. I got a daughter, and I'm killin' a nigga if she get taken advantage of. That wasn't your fault."

She smiled. "Thanks."

"For what?"

"For listening. Here." She handed him the half-filled bottle of liquor. "I've had enough. And I don't want to go home. Take me somewhere."

They ended up at the airport, lying on the hood of the Corvette, watching airplanes take off and land.

Dro sipped from the bottle of Patron. "This is the best date I've been on."

"Liar!" she laughed, pushing him playfully. "And this is not a date. We're just hanging out."

"Whatever you say. But I had a good time. You cool as hell when you let your guard down. Now that I know you, I like you."

"So, you like girls that cry, huh? Part of your game to comfort us?"

He laughed. "There is the Forever I first met."

She moved closer, laying her head on his shoulder. "Talk, Ruben. I just want to hear your voice."

"About what?"

"I don't care. Just talk."

"When I was little, I was crazy about airplanes. I wanted to learn how to fly them. Swore one day I would be a pilot and have my...."

The words trailed off in Forever's head, his voice vibrating in her ears as she watched his lips move. She didn't know what he was saying, but the smile on his face told her that he was reliving a good memory. Then something came over her and she got the strong urge to kiss him. The liquor had released inhibitions, and she grabbed his face and closed the distance.

Dro was surprised, but not for long. Their first kiss was soft and passionate. Places on his body got hard, and places on hers got wet. His hands roamed her body until they found the prize: her magnificent booty.

When he squeezed it, Forever panicked, pushing him. Hard.

"Oh shit!" he yelled before slipping off the hood of the car. "Ah! Shit, Forever! Damn," he cursed from the ground.

She scrambled from the hood of the car to help him up.

"I'm sorry, Ruben. I forgot about your leg. I didn't mean to kiss you, and I panicked."

"If you didn't mean to kiss me, why you kiss me? You tripping, girl."

"Look, Ruben, I like you. I can't even lie. But I can't go any further with you. I've been hurt, and I made a promise to God that I wouldn't date another man unless he was a Christian. I'm sorry if I led you on. I really like your company, and it feels good being around you. But I can't do this anymore."

Dro stared at her like she was crazy. "We back on this bullshit again?"

"You don't have to curse at me. This is what I want. I'm sorry."

Dro mugged her, not speaking for fear of disrespecting her. "You a trip," he mumbled before limping to the Corvette and getting in.

"Wait. Where are you going?"

He didn't answer, just started the car.

She ran to the passenger side and opened the door. "Ruben, what are –"

Her voice was drowned out by the radio. Bass pounded from the sub woofers, vibrating the car. She tried to scream over the music, but it was no use. When he put the car in gear, she finally got in. Rap music blared from the Corvette as he sped through the city traffic.

When he pulled up to her apartment building, he stopped in the middle of the street, not even looking at her, waiting for her to get out. She began screaming again, trying to get his attention. It was no use. He stared out the windshield, the bass pounding loud.

When she finally got out of the car, the Corvette's tires began spinning before speeding away.

Dro drove angrily through the Milwaukee streets, wishing he'd never met Forever. She was the epitome of bourgeois, and he hated stuck-up females. He didn't even want to think about her anymore, and the only way he knew to get a female out of his head was to get another one.

After parking behind America's Camry, he grabbed his .45 from the glove box, chirping the alarm on the Corvette as he used the crutches to hobble up the stairs. The door was unlocked, and he walked in, expecting to surprise his baby momma.

But when he walked in, he was the one who got a surprise. "Fuck is this shit?" he cursed, body growing warm with anger.

America shot to her feet, eyes wide with fear. "Wait, Dro! Let me explain!"

Asia sat on the couch next to a light-skinned nigga Dro had never seen before.

"Fuck this nigga doin' in here wit' my daughter? You know how we do, America. Ain't no niggas supposed to be in this house, especially around my daughter."

"I'm sorry, baby," she apologized, on the verge of tears. "This is my friend. I thought you were out of town."

Dro threw a crutch against the wall. "I don't give a fuck where you thought I was. Ain't no niggas supposed to be in here. You trick off wit' these niggas in the streets. Don't be bringing my baby into yo' bitch-ass games."

America found some courage. "This my house, nigga! And you ain't my daddy. I do what I want. I'm grown, nigga."

"You betta lower yo' voice before I put yo' lips on ice," Dro growled.

"Ay, brotha. That ain't no way to talk to a woman." The man stood, walking toward Dro.

America jumped between them. "Chris, this is–"

"Nigga, sit cho bitch-ass down!" Dro barked. "Matter fact, get the fuck out!"

He stood his ground. "This is America's house. She wants me here. I ain't going nowhere."

The .45 seemed to jump into Dro's hand like it had a mind of its own, barrel pointed at Chris' chest. "Nigga, get cho bitch-ass outta here before them people put you in a sandwich bag, fag!"

"No, Daddy!" Asia screamed.

"Don't, Dro. Please," America begged.

Chris looked like he was about to piss his pants. "C'mon, brotha. It ain't like that."

"I don't wanna rap, nigga. Get the fuck out."

Chris moved toward the door like he was The Flash.

"Asia, go to your room," Dro ordered.

"What the fuck is yo' problem, nigga? You can't be pulling guns out in front of Asia!" America snapped.

"If you wouldn'ta had that nigga in here, that shit wouldn't have happened. Don't try to put that shit on me. Fuck you bring that nigga in here for? I wasn't playin' when I told you don't bring no niggas in here."

"You ain't my man, Dro. You ain't finna be telling me what I can and can't do. If you gon' move in and be with me, then you can have some say. Otherwise, I don't wanna hear that shit."

Dro's face twisted into a mug. "That's how it is now? For real?"

"You know what I'm sayin', Dro. I love you, nigga. You know that. But I can't keep putting my life on hold because you don't wanna grow up. Damn, nigga. You run in and out of here like you live here and fuck me like I'm yo' girl, but you don't wanna commit. Ain't no tellin' how many bitches you out there fuckin', but you don't want me to fuck nobody. Damn, Dro. I wanna be happy, too. Can I live my life, too?"

"So, what, you choosin' that sucka-ass nigga over me? Is that what you trynna say?"

"Don't put no words in my mouth. You know that's not what I'm sayin'. I just want to be happy. I want to be in love. I want to be in a relationship with a man that wants only me."

He looked her up and down in disgust. "You trippin'. We had an agreement, and now you gettin' all brand new and shit. So, Chris make you happy? Got you changing up?"

"No. You make me happy. I wanna be with you. But if you can't be with me and only me, I'ma find somebody that can give me what I want."

Dro sank back against the wall, searching his baby mama's face. She wanted a man, to be in love, to get married. And he loved her, but wasn't in love with her. They tried to be together in the past, but it didn't work. They made better friends.

"A'ight. I'ma get my shit outta here tomorrow. Do you."

"Wait, baby!" America said, not expecting him to leave. "What are you doing?"

He hobbled over to grab his crutch. "Making the choice for you. I'm out."

Dro left America's house wondering how a good looking, 25-year-old nigga that had two cars, his own house, and money saved up could get rejected by two women in a matter of hours. "I shoulda went to Chicago," he mumbled, pulling into his driveway.

He had just walked in the house when his phone vibrated. It was a text from Forever. Just one word.

Sorry.

Reading it made him feel some type of way. He liked her more than he cared to admit. What he liked most about her was she wanted to push him to be better. When she found out about the preacher prophesying about the calling on his life, she wanted him to pursue it. He felt connected to her in a spiritual way. And he wanted to kiss her some more. Their lip-lock at the airport stirred something within, making him want her more, but she confused the hell out of him. One minute she was feeling him, the next she wasn't. And for some reason, the hot and cold was appealing.

So he did the unthinkable and hit her on FaceTime.

"Hey, Ruben," she answered, sadness in her eyes and voice.

"What up? I got the text."

"I'm glad you called."

"Listen, Forever. I don't know what it is about you, but you do something to me. I'm sorry for the way I acted earlier, but yo' hot-and-cold be throwing me. I was salty when you shot me down like that."

"I didn't shoot you down, Ruben. It wasn't like that."

He frowned. "Well, what you call it?"

"Okay, maybe I did. But that wasn't my intention."

"I hear you. I guess I gotta respect that you got standards or whatnot. You don't wanna compromise the promises you made with God. I get it."

A question shown in her eyes. "What brought on this understanding all of a sudden?"

He paused, wondering how much he should tell her. And as he looked into her eyes, he knew he couldn't lie anymore. If they had any chance at building something, it would have to be built on a solid foundation. "I went by my daughter's mother's house after I dropped you off. She had a nigga in there, and I snapped."

"What's wrong with her having a man in her house? I thought you weren't with her."

"Technically I'm not. But we still sleep together. We had an arrangement that we wouldn't bring our daughter around nobody we dealt with. She broke it tonight."

Realization flashed in her eyes. "Oh."

"After I snapped and kicked the nigga out, America gave me an ultimatum. Be with her or let her go. So I left."

"Why are you telling me this, Ruben? Why are you confessing your lies now?"

"Because I want you to know everything. You deserve the truth."

"So, there's more?"

Dro let out a long breath. "Yeah. There's more. I rob people for a living. Mostly drug dealers. And my leg is hurt because I got shot during a robbery."

Forever looked blown away. "Wow. I am. I don't know what to say. I thought you were a drug dealer. Wow," she said again before becoming silent. "Why didn't you tell me this before?"

"Because I want a do-over. Because I want to be with you."

J-Blunt

Chapter 11

"Mr. Patrick?"

Dro looked up from his phone toward the receptionist's desk. The skinny white woman with blonde hair smiled at him. "Yeah?"

"Mr. Feldman is ready to see you now."

After putting the phone in his pocket, he walked toward the door on the other side of the room.

Inside, a bald headed, light-skinned man was sitting at a desk going through papers. When Dro walked in, he stood, extending a hand. "Mr. Patrick, how are you? Have a seat. How can I help you?"

After shaking hands, Dro sat in the chair in front of the desk. "I'm okay. I need to find somebody. Well, two people."

He picked up a tablet. "Okay. Who do you need me to find? Do you have a picture, phone number, or last known address?"

"That's just it, man. I don't know who they are."

His brow wrinkled. "I'm a private investigator, not a miracle worker. What exactly do you want me to do?"

"I want you to find my friend's parents. Her name is Forever Mitchell. She was an orphan and never met them. I don't have any information on them. Not even a name."

He looked intrigued. "A real mystery, huh? Okay. Spell her name."

When he spelled it, Mr. Feldman typed on the tablet. "Whoa! She is a cutie. This her?" he asked, showing Dro the screen.

"Yeah. That's her."

"Okay. I can't make any promises because I don't have much to go on, but I'll look into it and see what I can do. It's going to be tough because she's an orphan, and sometimes the parents don't leave paper trails."

Dro nodded. "Okay. Just do what you can."

"I will. And as far as payment, I charge by the hour. And I'll need a contact number."

Dro pulled a wad of cash from his pocket and sat it on the desk. "That's five thousand. If that ain't enough, let me know. And I'll call you so you can have my number in your phone."

Mr. Feldman looked at the money and then back up at Dro. "I normally bill my clients after the job, but I don't mind an up front payment."

"Good, because I believe in prepayment. And you can keep the change."

The private investigator smiled. "That is very kind of you. I'll get on the case immediately. And I'll be in touch."

Dro left Mr. Feldman's office feeling hopeful. Forever was a beautiful person with a beautiful soul, and he wanted to do something nice for her. He was also hoping to get back on her good side.

It had been over a week since they last spoke. It turned out she couldn't handle the truth, and they agreed to go their separate ways. He didn't blame her. Her type didn't belong with someone like him. He was everything wrong in the world, and she was everything right. Oil and water. But that didn't stop him from thinking about her and wishing they could be more.

From the P.I.'s office he went to the hood. The Savages had gathered at Nu-Nu's house.

"Young Dro!" Lunatic called when he stepped from the Charger.

"'Sup wit' you niggas?" he asked, shaking hands with his niggas as he walked up on the porch.

"Shit. Posted. Looking at them hos move in down there," Tae said, nodding toward the moving truck on the corner.

"Anybody know 'em?"

"Nah," Nu-Nu spoke up. "But I'ma go find out who they is in a minute."

"Fuck them hos, Dro," Twenty said, shaking his head. "Them bitches the least of our worries. Niggas is hot," he said, shooting an accusing glance at Lunatic.

"What happened?"

"Luna sold that work to some niggas off the treys."

Dro didn't see the problem. "What's wrong with that? He got rid of it, right?"

"Them niggas buy work from Monster," Tae spoke up. "Luna sold that shit to them niggas for the low, and they put two and two together. Called Monster and told him. The niggas from the spot remembered him bustin' they nigga head wit' the gauge. They put 25 Gs on his head."

Dro looked at Luna. "They know you Savage?"

"Yeah. Somebody called Whisper and told him about the money on my head."

"Damn. We gotta fall back and stay out the hood for a minute," Dro said.

Tae mugged him. "Yeah right, nigga. Ain't no nigga finna make me hide. Fuck that! If them niggas want it, I'm givin' it out. Hot shit. Ain't no ho in me, nigga."

"On er'thang!" Twenty echoed. "Niggas gon' have to kill me, and that's hard as fuck. I'm a goblin, nigga."

"Plus one of Unc niggas opening a new club tonight, and he invited us. I'm goin'," Lunatic said.

"Me, too," Tae and Twenty echoed.

Dro didn't know what to say. His niggas had spoken, and it was situations like this that made him think he wouldn't live to see his thirtieth birthday. But they were brothers. Ride or die. Move in a pack like wolves. If a nigga came at one, a nigga came at them all.

"Say no more. It's on on-sight," Dro said, speaking with bravado he didn't feel.

After kicking it with his niggas, he got a call from Porscha, one of his old flames. She missed his dick, and he missed her pussy. Thirty minutes later he was standing on her porch, ringing the doorbell. She answered wearing a black nighty, looking like a sexy black panther

"I was wondering when you would come to your senses and come home," she purred, wrapping chocolate arms around his neck.

"You know I can't stay away too long," he grinned, letting his hands reacquaint themselves with her curves. Her Instagram name was Porscha The Body. She had over a million followers checking for the newest pictures of her crazy measurements. 36DD-26-50!

She grabbed his arm and pulled him into the house. "And I hope you brought a box of rubbers, nigga. I ain't had no dick in weeks."

They kissed their way to the couch, ripping at each other's clothes. When they were naked, Porscha took control, putting the rubber on him and climbing on top. She rode him hard, making him bust first. After putting a new condom on, she continued the ride, getting hers. Then he bent her over the couch and drilled her from the back, loving the way her big-ass booty bounced against his stomach.

Round three was in the bedroom. An hour later they lay in bed, smoking a blunt.

"Damn, Dro. It's some truth to absence making the heart grow fonder. I forgot how good the D was."

"You know I gotta put on a show when I come through," he bragged.

"Got me fuckin' these lame-ass niggas with lil'lil' dicks. Which is why you should come through more often. You still fucking with yo' baby mama?"

"Nah. She want that happily ever after shit. I ain't on none of that."

"Still ain't ready to turn in that playa card. I hear you. Play on, playa. I'm the same way. I'm too in love with chasing this check to be chasing a nigga."

"Preach!"

"But if you was the nigga I was chasing, I might reconsider," she laughed, biting him on the shoulder.

"Quit bullshitting. I seen yo' Instagram with Drake making it rain on yo' ass when you was in Atlanta. We go good together because you do you and I do me," he said before passing her the blunt.

"Yeah. But a bitch can dream, can't she?"

"Dream on, baby. Dream on."

"So, what are you doing next week? I'm flying out to Vegas for a couple days. I gotta dance at a club and do a photo shoot for a magazine. Wanna come? I need some good company and some good dick."

Dro thought for a moment. He could use a vacation to clear his head. The shit with Monster wasn't going to end well. Blood was going to get spilled. And if he was out of town when it happened, that wouldn't be a bad thing. But his niggas needed him. If something bad happened to one of them while he was gone, he wouldn't be able to forgive himself for not being there.

"Hello? Dro?"

"My bad," he laughed as his phone began vibrating. "I just zoned the fuck out." He checked the screen and seen a text from Lunatic. Whisper had them spots in the VIP.

"What's wrong?"

He sat the phone down. "Is it that obvious?"

"Written all over your face."

"My nigga uncle got us VIP spots at this club, but I really ain't trynna go."

"Well, don't go."

"It ain't that easy. Me and my niggas ride in packs. If they there, I'm there."

"See, that's what I don't understand about niggas. Who says y'all gotta follow the bro code or G code all the time? If you don't wanna do something, don't do it. It's your life."

"I wish it was that easy, baby."

"Why is it hard?"

"You wouldn't understand," he breathed.

"You probably right. You have too many secrets. Maybe that's why I like you so much."

"That and my good D," he cracked.

"Yeah. That, too. So, I guess I'll be going to Vegas alone?"

"Probably. But with your looks, you won't be lonely long."

She mugged him. "Nigga, did you just call me a ho?"

"C'mon, baby. You know I wouldn't come at you like that. But you do have over a million Instagram followers. I bet at least ninety percent of them is niggas. You won't be lonely, no matter where you go."

"It still sounds like you calling me a ho, but I understand what you saying. And FYI, I don't be fuckin' niggas that follow me on the 'Gram. I only fuck wit' a couple niggas: you, my east side nigga, and my football nigga in Atlanta."

"You know you don't gotta explain nothing to me. I rock with you the long way."

"I'm not explaining nothing. I'm just letting you know. So, what are you doing after the club?" she asked, rolling on top of him.

"Shit, if you want, I could be doing you."

"Good, 'cause I ain't going nowhere tonight. Just call before you come."

***

The parking lot of Vibes looked like a car show. Donks, trucks, and foreign whips on chrome filled the parking lot.

The candy-red Corvette rode slowly past the onlookers, bass vibrating the pavement. When Dro stepped from the car, he mugged the haters, saluted the players, and exchanged head nods with the women. He walked to the front of the line and said a few words to the bouncer before being allowed inside. After making his way to the roped-off section, he had a few more words with the security guard.

"Young Dro!" Lunatic screamed over the music, walking over with a bottle of Patron in one hand and a bottle of Ace of Spade in the other.

"What it do, nigga?" Dro grinned, grabbing the bottle of Patron.

"This muthafucka shakin', my nigga! I'm trynna leave wit' two or three hos!"

Dro looked around the VIP section and seen it was filled with fine women. The table Whisper, Tae, and Twenty was at had women sitting down and standing around it. That's where Dro headed.

"What took you so long, nigga?" Twenty slurred, handing him a bottle of liquor he'd never seen before.

"I was at The Body crib. Fuck you drinkin'?"

"Shit from Jamaica, nigga. Jamaican rum, boy!" He wobbled.

Dro sipped from both bottles, trying to catch up with his niggas. By the time the lights came up, signaling in was time to go, he was twisted, walking across the lot with a bad chick. Megan was Mexican, Laos, and black. And she was also bisexual.

"Call yo' girlfriend and let her know you met a real nigga wit' a big dick. And I love eating pussy."

"Dro, you are so crazy, nigga," she laughed.

"I know. Now let yo' fingers do the dialing."

They stopped at her blue Mustang so she could make the call. Dro scanned their surroundings while she talked to her girlfriend. Parking lot pimping was taking place, everybody looking for somebody to take home. Whisper's Cadillac limo caught his attention. Women were on top of the truck, stripping and dancing. A crowd gathered around to cheer and throw money. The Savages and Whisper were front and center.

Dro was about to turn back to Megan when a face in the crowd caught his attention. Monster. Next to him were two tall, light-skinned niggas. They were about fifty feet from the truck, watching and lurking.

"Shit!" Dro cursed, pulling out his cell and walking quickly toward his Corvette.

"Where you at, nigga?" Tae answered. "There hos out her gettin' it on!"

"Fuck them hos, nigga. Monster here!"

Tae's voice became instantly sober. "Where he at?"

"Behind y'all. In a crowd. He standing next to two tall, light-skinned niggas," Dro explained, popping the locks on the Corvette and pulling his .45 from the glove box. "Y'all strapped?"

"You know I don't go nowhere without my shit. But I can't see the niggas."

"They in the crowd. Tell Luna and Twenty. I'm strappin' up right now. I'm on my way over. If you see them niggas, shoot first. Stay dangerous."

"Already. Savage."

Dro was running toward the Cadillac limo when the shooting started.

Boom, boom, boom, boom, boom, boom!

Pop, pop, pop, pop, pop, pop, pop!

Clap, clap, clap, clap, clap!

Screams filled the night as the crowd dispersed in all directions. When he got to the scene, one of the light-skinned niggas was lying on the ground, blood covering the front of his shirt. A few feet away was Lunatic. He was lying on the ground, a pistol near him.

"You a'ight, nigga?" Dro asked, kneeling next to him and putting the pistol in his pocket.

"Nah, fam," he struggled. "Bitch-ass nigga shot me in the back. I can't move."

"Where Twenty and —"

Pop, pop, pop, pop!

Dro flinched, twisting and letting the .45 ride as he ducked behind the limo.

Boom, boom, boom, boom!

The second light-skinned nigga that was with Monster limped away. When Dro came back around the SUV, Whisper was pulling Lunatic into the limousine. Dro ran toward the Corvette, hoping he hadn't been recorded shooting.

Chapter 12

Dro hated courtrooms with a passion. The only thing he hated more than courtrooms themselves were the judges that ruled over them.

Today was Lunatic's arraignment. Dro, Tae, and Twenty sat in the back pew, trying not to be seen, but wanting to show support to their nigga. It had been a week since the club shooting. As soon as Lunatic healed from the surgery, he was arrested and locked up. Even though they didn't have a weapon because Dro picked it up and threw it in the sewer, they were still pinning the murder on Luna. Witnesses and cell phone video made him the shooter.

The Savages were lying low, seeing what they could do to get their brother out of the jam. If he got bail, they would pool their money and get him out.

At 11:00 o'clock on the dot, Lunatic was wheeled into the courtroom strapped to a wheelchair. This was the first time the Savages had seen him since the club, and besides the orange jumpsuit, he looked okay. He searched for his supporters as he was wheeled next to his lawyer. After waving to his mom and sisters in the front row, he nodded toward the Savages in the back.

When the proceedings began, the judge read off the charges: first degree homicide and possession of a weapon by a felon. The district attorney asked for no bail. Lunatic's lawyer, who was also Dro's lawyer, Brandon Williams, asked for a ten thousand dollar bail, arguing the case was self defense. The judge set bail at 150 thousand and banged his gavel.

"A hunnit fifty Gs! That's some bitch-ass shit," Dro cursed as he climbed in the Charger.

"Racist mu'fuckas," Twenty spat, climbing in the passenger seat. "If he was a white boy, he'da be out wit' self defense. Nigga got shot in the back and still get charged wit' a body. That's some racist shit."

"Nah, what's racist is them charging him with the body in the first place," Tae said from the back seat. "Y'all heard what the DA said. That nigga got shot wit' two guns. Luna hit him in the stomach with the nine, but the two .40 bullets to the chest killed him. Twenty the one that killed that nigga. And they ain't got no bangers, but they still charging him. That's some racist shit."

"We gotta bang Monster bitch-ass," Twenty said. "If my nigga facing life and go to the bing, we gotta whack that nigga. Life for a life."

"Let's suit up tonight," Dro nodded.

"Nah, we ain't gon' rush into nothing," Tae spoke up. "We gotta do our homework on this nigga. Find out where he live and hit them pockets before we leave 'im stankin'. We can't be on no reckless shit. This nigga ain't sweet, and his money long, so you know he got shooters."

"You right," Dro nodded. "Call Whisper and let him know we need to holla. He probably know where Monster lay his head."

***

"Yeah, I hear what you young hyenas is sayin', and as much as I want Monster in a box, I gotta look out for y'all. Gettin' that nigga ain't easy. He keep a couple shooters with him at all times," The Ho Whisperer said, blowing out a cloud of smoke.

Tae got heated. "Fuck that nigga, Whisper! We Savages. Don't no nigga put fear in us. We wreck shit. Don't try to save us. Save that nigga. He put a bounty on my nigga head, and we on his ass for that shit."

"Real shit," Twenty echoed. "That nigga tried to get us clapped up. Tell us where that nigga lay his head at so we can cut his shit off."

Whisper was quiet for a moment, looking around the living room at each Savage. After studying them for a moment, he smiled. "Let me put my ear to the streets and see what I come up with. I'ma get with y'all as soon as I know something."

***

Dro sat on the couch watching Black Panther for the hundredth time. Although it was his favorite action movie, he wasn't into it. He was thinking about life in the streets. Shit had gotten too real, and he could feel the jaws of death and prison getting closer. He hadn't been in the hood in a few days, staying home, smoking weed, and watching movies. He wanted to limit his risks of being shot and going to jail.

When the phone rang, he took his time answering. The screen read 'PI'.

"What's up, Mr. Feldman?"

"Hey, Ruben. I'm calling because I was able to gather the information you asked for. Do you think you could stop by the office?"

"Yep. Gimme about thirty minutes."

During the drive to the P.I.'s office, Dro was excited about the information he was about to receive.

When he walked in, Mr. Feldman stood eagerly to greet him. "Mr. Patrick, good to see you again."

"Same here. What you got for me?"

He picked up a manila envelope and handed it to Dro. "I have some good news. I found her parents."

"That was fast."

"Yeah. Turned out it was easier than I thought. And you overpaid me by thirty-seven hundred."

"Don't worry about it, man. Keep it. I might need your help later."

After leaving the P.I.'s office, Dro headed home with Forever on his mind. He hadn't spoken to her in a few weeks, and now that he had her parents' information, he couldn't get her off his mind. He wanted to call her so bad and be there to see her face when she opened the envelope, but they agreed to end their friendship, and he had to respect it.

He also respected her privacy, so instead of opening the envelope, he went to the post office and mailed it to her.

He had just pulled away from the post office when he got a call from Asia. "Hey, baby."

"Daddy, can you buy me a dog?"

"Why you want a dog? You don't even know how to take care of one."

"Because I need somebody to play with. Ever since you stopped coming over, I been bored."

"You know yo' mama ain't finna let you get a dog."

"She said I can have one, but she won't buy it. You gotta get it for me."

Dro wasn't convinced. "When did she say this?"

"Just now. That's why I'm calling you. I already picked out the puppy I want."

"Okay. I'ma come over later. We can talk about it then."

"No, Daddy! You gotta come now. I already picked out my dog. We gotta go get it before somebody else take it."

"Okay, okay. I'm on my way. Where yo' mamma?"

"In the living room with Chris."

He laughed. "Okay. I'm on my way. I'ma blow the horn when I'm outside."

After picking up Asia, he drove to the Humane Society where she picked up a two-month-old Boxer named Scooter. Next they went to a pet store to get him food and supplies. An hour later he was pulling up to America's house.

As soon as he parked at the curb, Asia leapt from the car with the puppy, running in the house.

"Hey! Come help me bring yo' dog stuff in the house!"

She ignored her father, too focused on her new best friend.

"Lil'Lil' brat!" he mumbled, getting out and pulling some of the dog's stuff from the trunk.

"Need some help?"

Dro looked up and seen America walking toward him, looking good. She wore tight white jeans that showed off her crazy figure, a gold halter top, and black leather boots.

"Somebody betta come help, 'cause that ain't my dog," he grumbled, pulling the thirty-pound bag of dog food onto his shoulder.

"I got you, baby daddy. So, you gon' help her train it?" she asked, pulling a bag of doggy toys from the trunk.

He let out a chuckle as he walked up on the porch. "That's you and Chris job."

"For real? That's how it is?"

He stopped, spinning to face her. "You tell me? Is that how it is?"

"You know it ain't like that. You the one that been avoiding me. Just come in so we can talk."

"We don't got nothing to talk about. We already said what we needed to say."

She pleaded with her eyes. "Dro, please. Just come in the house for a couple minutes."

After a short staredown, he walked in the house and sat the bag of dog food on the kitchen counter. "Where yo' boyfriend?"

"He left right after you picked up Asia. But forget him. I want to talk about us."

"I can't be the nigga you want me to be, America. We tried to be together, and you see how it worked out. We make better friends. You know it just like I do."

"But Asia want us to be together. We owe her that. I wanna give her what neither one of us had – a complete family. Don't you want her to have that?"

Dro smirked, unconvinced. "When we was together, all we did was argue and fight. I don't wanna go through that again. I love you and our daughter, but I can't give you what you want."

America's shoulders slumped, tears threatening to spill from her eyes. "So, that's it? After ten years, you just gon' walk away?"

"I'm not walking away. I'ma always be there for our daughter. But I'm giving you the opportunity to get what you want. I gotta go. I'ma holla at you later."

After saying goodbye to Asia, he left. During the drive home, he questioned if he made the right decision not getting back with America. There was a time when she was his baby and he was crazy about her, but he just wasn't feeling it anymore. Chris was probably what she needed. A man with a job who respected her. Dro's life was crazy, and the fewer strings attached to him, the better it was for everyone close to him.

By the time he made it home, he was at peace with the decision, but he did feel bad about the way he left America in the kitchen, crying. So he sent her a text.

Sorry.

She texted right back.

I know.

***

"We murkin' er'body in that bitch. No hesitation. No questions. Fuck that nigga whole family," Twenty breathed.

"Kids and all," Tae echoed. "Dogs, cats, er'body. Niggas gon' know not to fuck with Savages."

Dro sat on the couch in Tae's living room, loading 9mm bullets into the thirty-round clip. The Ho Whisperer had given the Savages four brand new Walter PP7s equipped with silencers. They planned on using them to bring death to Monster's doorstep. Everybody had to go.

As he used the rag to make sure no fingerprints were on the bullets, his phone ran. When he looked at the caller's name, he couldn't hide his surprise. "Hello?"

"Hey, Ruben," Forever said weakly.

"What's up? I wasn't expecting to hear from you. Kinda late, ain't it?" he asked, checking the time on his phone. It was 12:23 AM.

"I know. I can't sleep. How are you doing?"

"I'm a'ight. You calling about the envelope, huh?"

"Yes. Thank you so much. It's the nicest thing anyone has ever done for me."

"You welcome. I knew that not knowing where you came from was a big deal for you. I wanted to help you out and try to make amends for all the lies."

"Yeah, well, I kind of understood why you lied. I'm kind of a prude and can be really judgmental."

"For real? I never knew that about you," he laughed.

"Forget you, Ruben. I hope you get hit by another car."

"Damn. You seem more cruel since the last time we spoke. But I guess I deserved it. So, what was in the envelope? Were you able to get in contact with your parents?"

"You didn't open it?"

"Nah. That's between you and yo' people. I respect privacy."

"It was my mom's death certificate and my father's information. I think she died while giving birth to me. Her date of death is my date of birth."

Dro's mind was blown by the news. "Damn. That's crazy."

There was a brief moment of silence. "Ruben, can I ask you a question?"

The thought of what she would ask made him a little nervous. "Yeah. What you wanna ask me?"

She let out a long breath. "Since you helped me find my father, will you fly to North Dakota with me so I can meet him?"

The request surprised him, leaving him speechless.

"Ruben?"

"Yeah. Um, I'm here."

"Will you go with me? I don't want to go by myself."

"When do you plan on leaving?"

"The next plane leaves at four AM."

Dro glanced around the living room at his niggas. They were talking and loading their clips. The move would go down in another hour or so. He would be pushing it trying to

116

get to the airport by four o'clock, but Forever needed him, and he would be there for her.

"I'll meet you at the airport at 3:30."

"Who was that? America calling to get you back?" Twenty laughed after Dro hung up the phone.

"Nah. That was my alibi," he said, not wanting to tell them about Forever.

When the Savages were ready, they left Tae's house and hopped in a stolen black '90s-model Grand Am. They were dressed in all black with black leather gloves and Kevlar vests. The drive to Monster's suburban home was silent. They had made the drive several times in the last couple of days, casing the neighborhood to familiarize themselves with the surroundings.

During the drive, Dro thought about Forever. The call had surprised him. The request to fly to North Dakota with her was even more surprising. And he couldn't turn her down. No matter that he was about to murder an entire family, he would make time for Forever. She was his heart's true desire.

"A'ight. Here we go," Tae said, interrupting his thoughts.

They were two blocks from Monster's house, the suburban neighborhood covered in perfect darkness. After slipping on black surgical masks, the Savages climbed from the car and jogged through a couple yards until they were standing at the seven-foot wooden gate on the other side of Monster's back yard.

Dogs sniffed at the bottom of the gate. The pit bulls were killers, trained not to bark and attack silently. The Savages pulled their silenced pistols and let them ride, shooting through the gate. When the hammers hit the backs of the bullets, it sounded like someone being slapped. Whimpers and moans came from the wounded animals as they died.

Twenty bent down to look through the bullet holes. "We got 'em. Let's go."

The Savages cleared the gate, landing near three dying dogs lying in pools of blood. They raced across the back yard toward a sliding glass door. There was a camera to the right of the door next to brightly-shining security lights. The killers didn't care about being recorded because they wore masks.

When they got to the door, Tae raised his foot to kick it in. Right before he did, Dro stopped him and checked the door. To all of their surprise, it was unlocked.

When the goons were inside the house, they paused to listen and let their eyes adjust to the darkness. They knew Monster had live-in shooters, so they took a moment to strategize.

"I'ma check the back," Tae whispered. "Twenty, you check the front. Dro, check upstairs. Kill er'body. Stay dangerous."

"Savage," Dro and Twenty echoed before going on their missions.

Dro took his time moving up the stairs. On the way, he could hear the silenced pistols clapping again. Tae or Twenty had made kills. When he got to the top of the stairs, he paused to look down the hall. There were four doors, all of them closed. He moved slowly to the first one, his heart beating so loud he thought he would wake the people sleeping.

After opening the door, he peeked inside. It was an empty bathroom.

Another door was across the hall. Dro poked his head in the bedroom, and with the help of the moonlight he was able to see inside. Children's toys were scattered across the floor.

There were two beds near the window. He crept in and seen two little girls sleeping.

Tae and Twenty's words about killing everyone in the house played in his head. He lifted the pistol to the closest girl's head, applying pressure to the trigger. Then thoughts of him checking on Asia while she slept popped into his head. He tried to push his baby girl from his head, but couldn't. It wasn't in him to kill kids.

After wrestling with his thoughts for a moment, he left the room, closing the door behind him. He moved to check the next room when he noticed something was different. The door next to the girls' room was ajar. When he came upstairs, all the doors were closed.

Thinking someone was in the room calling the police, he moved quickly. Right when he was about to walk in the room, his cell phone vibrated in his pocket, scaring the shit out of him and making him jump.

Boom!

Dro's body was lifted from the ground and slammed into the wall across the hall as the shotgun slug punched him in the chest. The pistol flew from his hand as he crumpled to the floor, struggling to breathe. He looked toward the door and seen a hole in it the size of a basketball. Then there was the unmistakable sound of a shotgun coughing a shell onto the floor as another round was chambered.

Dro couldn't believe he wasn't dead, but knew he had to move before the shotgun wielder came into the hall. He gasped for air, trying to lift himself up from the floor. It was a struggle because his right arm wouldn't move.

The hinges on the door got his attention. It opened slowly, and a second later he was staring down the barrel of a shotgun. Visions of his mom, sisters, America, and Asia flashed in his mind.

Clap, clap, clap, clap, clap, clap!

The man stumbled backward before falling to the floor. Twenty sprinted past and into the room to make sure he was dead.

Tae kneeled next to Dro and helped him stand. "You a'ight, Dro?"

"Nah, Tae. Nigga shot me!" Dro moaned, touching his chest. The slug lodged into the vest like it had been welded on. He couldn't believe the slug didn't rip through the vest. It was a miracle.

"I got that bitch. You good?" Twenty asked when he walked out of the room.

"Yeah. Go check that last room," Dro nodded toward the door at the end of the hall.

"C'mon, Twenty. Monster wasn't downstairs. Let's get him!"

Dro was struggling to bend down and pick up his pistol when the silenced pistols began clapping again. Whoever was in the room fired back before everything went quiet.

And that's when Dro noticed the girls' bedroom door was cracked open, two sets of eyes staring at him. He staggered toward the room as the door slammed shut. When he walked in the room, the girls were whimpering in the corner, holding onto each other for dear life.

Then they began screaming.

He lunged at them, hurting his entire body as he reached out to cover their mouths. "Shut the fuck up! Shut up! Y'all bet not scream again or I'ma kill y'all ass!" he threatened.

The girls whimpered some more, but didn't scream.

"Get in the closet! Hurry up! And be quiet," he ordered, glancing toward the door, praying Twenty or Tae didn't walk in the room.

The girls did as they were told. After closing the door, he limped from the room as Tae and Twenty came out of Monster's room. Twenty carried a bulging pillowcase.

"Who was that screaming?" Tae asked.

"I had to kill his kids," Dro lied.

Twenty looked amused. "Straight up?"

Dro answered the question with one of his own. "Did y'all get that nigga?"

"Hell yeah!" Tae smiled. "Him and wifey. Let's get the fuck up outta here."

J-Blunt

Chapter 13

Dro walked slowly through the airport, the pain in his chest threatening to bring him to his knees. The Percs he had gotten from Twenty did nothing to mask the pain. Several times during the ride to meet Forever he thought about turning around and going to the hospital. Something inside was broken and bleeding. It literally hurt to breathe. But his desire to keep his word and not wanting to be in the hospital with wounds from a gunshot after a quadruple homicide powered him on.

When he spotted her near the terminal rocking jeans, a t-shirt, and Nikes, some of the pain left his body.

"Hey, Ruben!" she smiled, reaching out to hug him. "I was wondering when you would show up. You didn't pack anything?"

"Nah. I'll buy what I need when I get there. Ssh! Ah, shit!" he grunted when she hugged and squeezed him.

She jumped back, concern spreading on her face. "What's wrong? Are you okay?"

"Yeah. I'm good," he lied, wiping sweat from his brow.

She continued to stare at him. "No, you're not. You're hurt again. What happened?"

"I'm good. Let's get on the plane."

They didn't talk during the flight because as soon as Dro sat in the seat, he went to sleep. Forever was mad that he lied to her, and her mind thought the worst. She could only imagine how he got injured. The last time she seen him, he was on crutches because he got shot. This time he almost cried when she hugged him. Questions swirled through her mind, but she couldn't ask because he was asleep.

Sweat covered his body, and he constantly fidgeted. She had never seen anyone having a nightmare, but was sure he was having one. And it looked to be getting worse by the minute.

Then his eyes shot open like he had been scared awake. "Ah, shit!" he groaned, grabbing his side as he sat up.

"Are you okay?" Forever asked, watching him like he was possessed by an evil spirit.

He wiped sweat from his forehead. "Yeah. I'm good."

"No, you're not. Tell me what's wrong. I'm not playing."

He lay back in the seat gingerly. "It was a bad dream."

She scolded him like a mother did her child. "Stop lying to me. I'm not talking about the dream. I'm talking about your body. Where is it hurting?"

He let out a pained breath. "All over."

"What happened?"

"Work-related injury."

She didn't think the joke was funny. "Stop playing with me. You don't have a job."

He glanced at her. "I work in repo, remember?"

She connected the dots in her mind, eyes growing wide. "Oh my God! You got shot again?" she asked, way louder than necessary.

Panic spread on his face. "Shh! You can't be talking about shootings on airplanes," he whispered.

After realizing her mistake, she looked around to see if anyone was listening. She didn't see any obvious eavesdroppers, so she lowered her voice and continued the interrogation. "Were you shot again?"

"Nah. But it feels like it."

She got mad. "What is that supposed to mean?"

"We ain't about to talk about it right now. People might be listening."

She looked around the coach section again. There were lots of people within earshot. Even if they acted like they weren't listening, they were so close that they would hear. So she left him alone. For now.

Dro eventually dozed back into a fitful sleep, and she watched him the entire time. Her mind ran wild while he slept. She wondered if bringing him along was a mistake. He had been shot twice since they met. Then she thought about how many people he'd shot. Had he killed? Did he hurt women and children?

Two hours later the pilot announced their landing. When Dro opened his eyes, she was staring at him.

"What?"

"Are you okay?"

"You worry too much. I'm good," he winked.

She shook her head, buckling her seatbelt. "I don't know what I'm going to do with you."

"Can you buckle me up? It hurts when I move my arm."

She buckled him in angrily. "That's it. When we land, you're going to the hospital. And I'm not arguing with you about it."

***

Grand Forks, North Dakota was a small, white town that seen gun violence every couple of years. The town had only seen ten murders in the past thirty years. Which was why Dro wasn't about to tell the emergency room nurse he got shot.

"Where does it hurt?" the woman asked, looking at his chart.

"Everywhere. My chest and ribs. I got hit by a truck right before I got on the plane. I think something broke."

Her eyes popped. "You got hit by a truck? How?"

"I was running across the parking lot. I was rushing because we were late. Didn't see the truck, and the driver didn't see me. I thought it was just a little bump until mid-flight."

"Take your shirt off so I can take a look."

"I don't think I can do that. It hurt to move my arm."

She lifted the right side of his shirt to take a peek. A bruise with all the colors of the rainbow covered most of his torso. "Oh, man! This is nasty," she admitted, pulling a pair of scissors from the drawer. "I'm going to have to cut your shirt off."

When she cut the fabric from his body, a massive bruise covered his chest and rib cage on the right side. "Oh my God!" Forever mumbled, covering her mouth.

"I'm going to have to move your arm a little. Tell me if it hurts," the nurse said before trying to lift his arm

"Ah! That hurts."

"Where?"

"My ribs, mostly."

She touched the bruise on his ribs and he almost jumped off the exam table. "Ah shit!"

"Looks like your ribs are broke. I'm gonna have the doctor order x-rays. We'll also need to check for any continued internal bleeding. Flying on an airplane may have made the bleeding worse. Hang tight. I'll be back."

When the nurse left, Forever got on his ass. "What happened? And you better not lie to me. Tell me the truth."

"I got shot in my vest."

She got angry. "When are you going to stop? How many times do you need to get shot before you realize you need to change your life? What about your daughter?"

He got on her level. "Chill with the lectures, shorty. You overstepping."

126

She got angrier. "Why? Because I don't want you to get killed? How is that overstepping? You have a child, Ruben. That girl needs you. The best you. Not the shot up, dead, or in jail you. You're not a stupid thug. You're smart enough to know the life you're living is not the life God wants you to live. You said you believe God has a calling on your life. The preacher told you. God is keeping you around for a reason. Don't you want to live to see what it is?"

Dro thought on her words for a moment. Everything inside him knew she was right, but he still resisted. "You don't get it, Forever. I can't just walk away. This what me and my niggas do. How we eat."

"But anything is better than getting shot or dying, right? Why do you do it? For the money? I'm sure you can think of another way to survive. And what good is having money if you don't live to spend it?"

The doctor walked back into the room with the nurse, halting their conversation. "Did you really get hit by a truck before your flight?" the doctor asked.

After getting X-rays and a CT scan, they diagnosed Dro with cracked ribs and deep tissue bruising, prescribing him Oxycotin and a brace to protect his ribs. By the time they got to the hotel, he was heavily medicated and passed out on his twin bed.

While he was asleep, Forever got a rental car and went to buy food. Since he didn't pack a bag, she stopped to buy him a t-shirt, underwear, and some hygiene items. When she got back to the hotel, she ate before climbing into her own bed and trying to fall asleep.

It didn't work. Even though it was eleven o'clock in the morning and she hadn't slept in more than 24 hours, she wasn't tired. Thoughts of Ruben and meeting her father played in her head. Two men. So many questions. She thought about calling the number the P.I. provided. It was supposed to be her father's number, but she didn't know what to say or what he would say, which was why she wanted to look in his face first. Look for any resemblance. See if his eyes lit up when she told him she was his daughter. Make it personal. And she wanted Ruben there for support. So she lay in bed, trying not to overthink.

To take her mind off the men, she watched TV and played games on her phone. Late in the afternoon, Ruben stirred.

"What time is it?" he asked, struggling to sit up in bed.

"Almost five o'clock. They gave you the good stuff, huh?"

He smiled. "Had me in the clouds. But it ain't taking the pain away," he groaned, getting up from the bed and limping to the bathroom.

"How do you feel?" she asked when he came out.

"I'ma live. And I'm hungry. And I need to get a shirt and get outta this hospital shit."

She pointed to bag sitting on the table. "I got you some Chick-Fil-A and personal items. None of it is name brand."

He checked the bags and pulled out the chicken sandwiches. "Thanks. Labels don't make me. I make the label. Did you call him?"

"No. I can't.'"

"You really just wanna pop up on his doorstep? What if he got a family? What if it's a bad time? What if he not there?"

"I thought about all that while you were asleep, and I need to see him when I tell him for the first time. I know it doesn't make sense, but it's what I want to do."

"A'ight. However you want to do it, I'll be right there. What time you wanna go?"

"Within the next hour or two. If he works, give him some time to get home. Plus, you need to shower."

They left the hotel at six o'clock, using the rental car's GPS to find the address. It was a nicely-kept green-and-black one-story house in the middle of the block.

After parking, Forever began having doubts.

"What if he doesn't accept me?"

"He will. Give him a chance."

She spun to face Dro, fear in her eyes. "But he never looked for me all these years. What if he stayed away on purpose?"

"We didn't come all this way for nothing. It's okay to be scared, but I got you. You don't got nothing to lose. You are an amazing woman. If he don't wanna see you, it's his loss."

She stared at him for a few moments before a smile spread across her face. "Thanks, Ruben. For everything. I really mean it. I'm ready."

The butterflies in her stomach went crazy as they approached the house. Whey they were on the porch, she took a deep breath before looking to Dro. He nodded, encouraging her to ring the doorbell. Her hand moved slowly toward the white button.

The chime sounded.

"Who is it?" a deep voice called from inside the house.

"Um, Forever. Is Spencer Hawkins here?"

There were a few moments of silence before locks clicked and the door opened. A brown-skinned man with a short salt-and-pepper afro peered at them through the screen door. He had a large forehead, wide nose, full lips, and graying goatee. He looked at Forever and Dro suspiciously.

"I'm Spencer. How can I help you?"

"Hi, Spencer," Forever began, her voice shaking a little. "My name is Forever, and I think you're my father."

He frowned like she slapped him in the face. "I beg your pardon?"

She repeated what she said, feeling more confident the second time. "I think I'm your daughter."

He gave her a hard stare before turning to Ruben. "If this is some kind of game –"

"This ain't no game, sir," Dro spoke up. "We just flew all the way from Milwaukee to meet you. Forever is yo' daughter."

Spencer stepped onto the porch, astonishment drawn across his face "My daughter? How?"

"Kim Wong is my mother. Was my mother," Forever explained, pulling out the death certificate.

Spencer took the piece of paper and studied it like it was a map before looking at Forever again. "Kim was your mother? My goodness, you look just like her. What happened to her? How did she die?"

"I don't know. I was hoping you could tell me."

He looked dumbfounded. "I don't know. I haven't seen her in almost thirty years."

"Well, her date of death is my date of birth. I think she died while having me."

He looked at the piece of paper again. "Jesus!" he mumbled. "But wait, I can't be your father. She was with another guy."

"What other guy? Your name is all I got."

He paused to think for a moment. "This is a lot for me to process right now. Y'all come in. Can I get you some drinks? I need a beer."

"I'm okay," Forever said.

"I'll have what you having," Dro said.

"And who are you, young man?" he asked after closing the door.

130

"I'm Ruben, a friend of Forever's."

"He's the one who helped me find you," she said.

"Okay. Y'all have seats. I'ma go get those beers."

When Spencer left the room, Dro noticed the worried look on her face. "It's okay. Everything is going to be alright. You look like him a little."

She was on the verge of tears, but held her composure. "I know. It just feels surreal."

Spencer came back in the living room with two beers and a look of disbelief on his face "Here you are, son. I'm sorry, Forever, but this is a lot to take in. How old are you?"

"I'm twenty-eight."

He did the math in his head. "Yeah, that was about the last time I seen Kim. But she didn't tell me she was pregnant. What did your family say?"

"I don't know them. I grew up in foster homes."

Spencer looked like his heart broke. "Wow. I don't even know what to say."

"Can you tell me the other man my mom was with, just in case?"

"Yeah. His name is Ken. I think his last name was Mitchell."

"That's my last name."

"The thing about Ken is, he's white. And you don't look white to me."

"I second that," Dro cut in.

"I can't figure out why she wouldn't tell me she was pregnant. Where were you born?"

"Right here in Grand Forks."

He looked blown away. "You mean to tell me that you were raised right here in North Dakota? All this time we were in the same state?"

Forever looked just as surprised as the old man. "I guess so. What happened between you and my mom? Why did you break up?"

"Your mother came from a traditional Chinese family. Strict values. Kim was twenty-three years old and in college, but her parents still gave her an eleven o'clock curfew. Even on the weekends. I met her after her bike caught a flat tire. Gave her a ride home, and the rest is history. We messed around for about six months before her parents found out. Pretty Chinese girl with a black man wasn't her parents' American Dream for their daughter. They put pressure on her to stop seeing me. Even threatened to shun her. I loved your mother, but I didn't want to be the reason she split with her family. I was an active duty Marine and used to leave for months at a time. We weren't ready to get married, so I couldn't take her overseas with me. With everything that was going on in our lives, I broke it off with her. A little while later, I heard she was with Ken."

Forever looked like she wanted to cry. "Wow. That sounds like it was rough."

"It was. She was a good woman. Kind-hearted. Would help anybody. She was special."

"Do you have any pictures of her?"

"No. No, I don't. Sorry."

"It's okay. So, what do you think we should do?"

Spencer took a deep breath and let it out slowly. "Well, the first thing I want to do is tell you I'm sorry for not being there for you. I didn't know she was pregnant. She never told me. And the next thing I want is a hug."

***

"Pink pajamas, huh?" Ruben laughed, struggling to take off his shirt.

Forever walked out of the bathroom wearing a pink nightgown. "I love pink. You don't like?" she asked, striking a pose.

"You make everything look good. But you could rock one of those bed sheets and make it fly."

She blushed. "Aw. You're so sweet. Let me help you take this off. Lift your arms."

After finally getting the shirt off, he sat on his twin bed. "So, how are you doing? How do you feel about meeting your father?"

She couldn't contain her smile as she sat next to him. "I feel amazing. I know where I came from, and it has answered a lot of my questions. I mean, we won't find out 'til tomorrow if he's really my dad, but I feel good. Thank you for doing this for me. And for coming with me."

"I just wanted to make you happy. And I'm glad I could be here to share this with you. I like being around you. I can't remember the last time I had a peaceful day like this. No shoot-outs, police, or watching the faces of everybody I walk past. The time I got to spend with you and yo' pops was special."

"Awe! So, you do have a soft spot."

"Only when I'm with you. And you bet not tell nobody," he laughed.

Forever looked like she wanted to say more, but hesitated. Dro waited. Instead of using her voice to express what she wanted to say, Forever let her lips do the talking, leaning forward and pecking him on the lips. The kiss turned into a full-blown make-out session, and their bodies became intertwined. When she lay back on the bed, she pulled Dro on top, spreading her legs and revealing she wasn't wearing panties.

Dro's dick was so hard he thought it would bust through his boxers and pants as he dry humped. When he realized what they were doing, he broke the kiss, not wanting a repeat of what happened at the airport. "Wait, Forever. You sure you want to do this?"

She stared up at him with hot lust in her eyes. "You make me feel so good, Ruben. I want to feel all of you. I'm ready."

That was all he needed. He had been wanting her since the moment he laid eyes on her, so going to get a condom never crossed his mind. And he was leaving the lights on so he could see everything.

While he stood to undress, she pulled the nightgown over her head, revealing a body that made him pause. Dro stared at her for a moment, committing her body to memory. Her breasts were full and perky, dark nipples pointing like little missiles, stomach flat, waist slim, hips wide and inviting. And the sight of her pussy made him salivate. The skin tone the same as the rest of her body, the hair trimmed low. He couldn't wait to taste it as he climbed on top, kissing her lips before working his way to her breasts and down her body.

"Oh, Ruben!" she moaned as he placed kisses between her thighs. "Shh! Oh, my God! Ruben! Oh, my God!" she called repeatedly when he began licking her clit.

For Dro, her moans sounded like angels singing, tickling his ears and encouraging him to perform.

It only took a few moments for her body to begin shivering and locking up. "Oh, Ruben! Oh, Ruben!" she screamed as years of pent-up desire was released from her womb.

When he kissed his way back up her body, he noticed the tears spilling from her eyes. "You good?" She nodded, unable to speak. Tears during sex was new to him, so he wasn't sure how to react.

Forever grabbed his tool and pulled him to her pussy, moaning when he slipped inside. Dro paused, caught between the ultimate pleasure and pain. His ribs were killing him from her tight embrace, and her insides had him wondering if it was possible for pussy to feel this good. She had the perfect wetness, tightness, and warmth.

After letting her adjust to him, he went to work, starting with slow shallow strokes. A few moments later he was deep in her guts with long strokes. Forever loved every moment of the passion, losing herself in the moment, giving everything and wanting more. And Dro gave his all, hammering away at her pussy like it was his last fuck before doing a life bid.

She came again. He came soon after. But they weren't done.

"Roll over," he told her, reaching for a pillow and setting it under her pelvis, tooting her ass up just right. He admired her perfect backside for a moment before slipping back inside her sugary walls.

Forever went mad beneath him, loving the pleasure he gave. He kissed her cheek, the back of her neck, bit her shoulder, and nibbled her ear while rocking her world. The pleasure was more than she'd ever felt, giving her another orgasm.

After busting his second nut, he knew leaving America was the right decision. Dro had finally found the one.

***

"That was amazing!" Forever smiled, leaning forward to kiss her lover.

"You are amazing," Dro said, returning the kiss.

"You are a really amazing guy, you know that?"

"I always knew that. But tell that to the nigga that shot me," he cracked.

"I'm serious, Ruben. After getting to know you, it's hard to believe you rob people and get shot. You're smart, funny, warm, and caring. Like you come from a good home."

"I do come from a good home. My mom and step pops good people. I was raised in church, remember?"

"What happened? How did you get so bad?"

"I got my first taste of the street life when I was ten. My pop got killed in a robbery when I was a baby, and moms didn't want me in the streets and tried to keep me in the house. When I met my nigga, Twenty, he introduced me to his cousin, Deuce. He was a big, crazy, cock-eyed dude that always carried guns. He let us play with his TEC-9 that day, and it gave me a rush like I never felt before. I got hooked on guns, and the street life after that."

"Have you been to prison?"

"Yeah. When I was eighteen. Did a year and a half for serving an undercover police."

"Have you ever shot anyone?"

He looked in her eyes. "You really want me to answer that?"

She held his stare. "Yes."

"Yeah."

"How many people?"

"More than one. But I don't talk about the dirt I did in the streets. The G-Code."

She laughed. "Stop playing."

His look was serious. "I'm for real, Forever. You know I'm feeling you, but I don't talk about my dirt. I never told none of this to my daughter's mother. She don't know how I get money. That's how we do it in the streets. The less people that know what you do, the better."

She was quiet for a few moments. "Do you want to stop one of these days?"

"I've been thinking about it a lot lately. I keep getting shot, and I feel like God is trying to tell me something."

"Maybe He is. You keep getting shot and going to jail. I think God is warning you it's time to stop."

"I talked to my uncle about this a lot."

"So, when are you going to stop?"

He let out a long breath. "I don't know."

She pressed a hand against his sore rib.

"Ah!" he flinched. "What you do that for?"

"Because I want you to stop being stupid."

"I always told myself I would stop when I got a hunnit Gs. I spent that three or four times already. My lifestyle is expensive."

She frowned, curiosity getting the best of her. "How much money do you have?"

"About thirty."

Her eyes popped. "Thousand?"

"Yeah."

"That's more than enough to walk away. You can start a business, or at least invest in one."

"I can't walk away now."

"Why not?"

"You wouldn't understand."

"I've been very understanding since I met you. Try me."

"Nah, I can't."

"Why?"

"Because the streets is all I know. I don't know how to do nothing else."

"I'll help you."

He looked at her and smirked. "Yeah, right."

She sat up in bed to look him in the eyes. "If you give me your word you'll stop robbing people and turn your life around, I'll give you my word that I'll help you. You don't have to do it alone. I'm your friend. You helped me, now it's my turn to help you."

Dro became silent. Thinking.

"Think about your daughter, Ruben. Don't let her grow up like I did, without a father. She needs you to live. I promise to be by your side. I need you to live."

Seeing the tears threatening to spill from her eyes got to him. She was a good girl. Everything he never knew he wanted in a woman. His woman. "Okay. I give you my word."

Forever smiled like she won the lottery, leaning in to kiss him again. "I want to smother you in my arms so bad."

"You bet not touch my ribs again," he warned.

"I'm not going to hurt you, scaredy cat. But I need to ask you one more thing."

"Okay. What up?"

"Have you been saved?"

He frowned, wondering how they'd gone from kissing to discussing salvation. "What kinda question is that?"

"Have you confessed your sins and asked Jesus to be your personal Lord and Savior?"

He shrugged. "I think I did when I was little."

"Do you want to be saved?"

He frowned. "I don't know. I guess so."

"Yes or no, Ruben?"

"Yeah."

"Good. Because I told God my next man would be a Christian. Recite the sinner's prayer with me."

Chapter 14

Dro was awakened by his bladder demanding to be emptied. He reluctantly unwrapped Forever's arms from around him and made the painful attempt to get out of bed. It took a while, but he managed to get up and limp to the bathroom.

After draining the snake and washing his hands, he grabbed his phone and checked the time. It was 1:23 p.m. Not wanting to wake Forever, he stepped in the bathroom to check messages, missed calls and texts. The one that demanded his attention was a call from Asia.

"Hey, baby. What up?"

"Where you at, Daddy? Why didn't you call me yesterday? You supposed to call me every day, remember?"

"I know. I'm out of town. Sorry."

"You out of town? Where?"

"North Dakota."

"Why you all the way over there?"

"I came with my friend. She wanted to look for her father."

"Oh. So, when you coming back home?"

"Tonight or tomorrow. Why?"

"Because me and Scooter miss you. We want to come by your house."

"Okay. I'ma pick y'all up as soon as I get back."

"Okay. I'ma call you later. You better answer the phone."

He couldn't help but laugh. "Who you think you talkin' to like that? Betta calm down before I snatch the bones out of yo' body."

"Please, Daddy. You don't want these problems. I'ma call you later. Bye."

He laughed and shook his head after she hung up. Asia was getting way too grown. He was about to leave the bathroom when the phone vibrated. It was a jail call.

"What it do, Luna?"

"Young Dro! What's good, my nigga?"

"Shit. Livin' this savage life. How you holdin' up in there?"

"You know it don't matter where they put a real nigga at. We gon' make it on the moon or at the bottom of the ocean. This jail shit don't stop nothin'."

"Real shit. Hold yo' head up in that bitch. Do you need me to send you some shit? One of them care packages?"

"Nah. You know Whisper making sure a nigga straight. I was just callin' to see what yo' ass was up to. I miss you niggas, no homo."

"I see jail done made you sensitive. Gettin' in touch with yo' emotions while you in there?" he cracked.

"Fuck you, ol' T.D. Jakes-watchin'-ass nigga. I know you be crying when you get the Holy Ghost."

"That shit was weak as fuck," Dro laughed. "You been watchin' the news?"

"Hell yeah. I seen y'all. On to the next one."

"We did that. So, what up with the case? Why they ain't trynna give you self defense?"

"I don't know, but Brandon on the DA ass. Right now we trynna get this bail dropped. I got a hearing coming up. Brandon trynna get it down to fifty."

"And you know we got you when they do that."

"I wouldn't expect nothing else. I need a blunt and some pussy bad as a mu'fucka."

After kicking it with his boy for the fifteen minute call, Dro climbed back in bed with Forever and got some wake-up sex.

140

They ended up spending another day in North Dakota so Forever could take a paternity test.

***

"Make sure you call me later," Forever smiled, climbing into her truck.

"I will. I wanna hear you speak in tongues again like you did last night."

She shook her head, a sparkle in her eyes. "You are a mannish little boy."

"And you a mannish little girl. Now gimme a kiss and get outta here."

After another lip-lock, Forever drove away and he walked to his Charger. He had just climbed inside when the phone rang. It was Twenty.

"What it do?"

"Damn, nigga. We thought something happened to you. Fuck you ain't been answering the phone?"

"I was outta town and left my phone in my car at the airport," he lied. "I just got back."

"Oh yeah?" Twenty asked skeptically. "Did you holla at Tae and get yo' cut of that move?"

"Nah. I'm leaving the airport right now. What we get?"

"Three hunnit Gs."

Dro's eyes popped. "Three hunnit racks? On what?"

"On everything I love, nigga. We split it seventy-five apiece. We already gave Luna share to Whisper for bail. He got a hearing tomorrow. They trynna get it dropped to fifty. If they do, we gettin' him out."

Dro smiled. "Damn, that lick was right on time. I can't wait to see my nigga. 'Bout time something good happened for us for once."

Twenty's tone changed. "Er'thang ain't good, Dro."

He noticed the vocal change. "What you mean by that?"

"Them girls. What the fuck, Dro? Er'body was supposed to get it, nigga."

He let out a long breath. "I couldn't do it, brah. I couldn't do no shorties like that."

"That shit all over the news, nigga. Mu'fuckas talkin' 'bout that shit online and all kinds of shit. You know Twelve talked to the kids. What if that shit come back to bite us, nigga? You knew the move before we went in."

"But them was kids, my nigga. And they didn't see shit. We was masked up."

"Yeah, I hope so. But if that shit come back to bite us, it's on you."

Dro didn't like what he was implying. "Fuck that s'posed to mean?"

"You know exactly what I'm sayin', nigga. You fucked up. It is what it is. Tae heated about that shit, too. Heads up."

"Yeah, a'ight," Dro breathed. "Let me go home and get right. I'ma get wit' you niggas later. Stay dangerous."

"You know it. Savage."

Dro drove home thinking about the conversation with Twenty. He fucked up not killing the kids. If they got caught, the blame was on him. He still wasn't sure how he felt about it, but he didn't like it. Nor did he regret the decision to let the girls live. He wasn't killing kids.

After convincing himself he did the right thing, he went in the house to shower. He thought about the thirty thousand in his safe and the seventy-five he would add to it. A hundred Gs wasn't a lot of money, but for somebody that was leaving the street, it was a hell of a prize to walk away with. His next goal was to figure out a way to make the money grow. No way he could survive off a hundred thousand. He could spend that in a couple days. He also had to figure out what would become of him and Forever. They hadn't talked about being together. Yet. But he promised he would call her later. For now he had to get the rest of his money.

After the shower, he got dressed and drove to see Tae. "Fuck you ain't been answering yo' phone?" Tae mugged.

"I was outta town and forgot my phone in the car at the airport," Dro lied as he walked in the house.

Tae's mug got meaner. "See you still lyin', nigga. Luna said he talked to you yesterday. Fuck you on?"

Dro let out a breath. "I don't feel like doin' this with you, brah. Lemme get my paper so I can bounce."

"Nah, nigga. We gotta address this. Fuck you ain't get them lil'lil' hos out the way? You know what the move was. Er'body was s'posed to get it. Kids. Dogs. Er'body!"

"I wasn't killin' no kids, Tae. They didn't have nothin' to do with that shit."

"That wasn't the point, nigga. We wasn't leaving no witnesses. Now, what if them lil'lil' bitches seen or heard some shit that get us knocked? Then what? You still gon' be on this same 'I ain't killin' no kids' shit when you locked in a cell for the rest of yo' life, nigga?"

Dro didn't like Tae's aggressive tone or demeanor. "Aye, nigga, I ain't yo' shorty! Lower yo' voice and take some of that bass out."

Tae got louder. "Nah, nigga! You fucked up and I'm lettin' you know 'bout it. I don't give a fuck 'cause you in yo' chest, nigga. You put us all at risk by bitching up. You shoulda killed them kids."

Dro was beyond pissed and knew he needed to leave before he busted Tae in his shit. "Dawg, you got one more time to disrespect me. Gimme my bread so I can ride."

Tae looked him over from head to toe like he was disgusted by Dro's presence. "I shouldn't give yo' soft ass shit, nigga."

The anger took over and Dro lost it, taking a swing at Tae, connecting with his jaw. Tae stumbled, recovering quickly and landing a punch of his own. The goons squared up and began exchanging blows. Dro was taller with longer arms, so he landed the most. Tae evened the match by turning it into a wrestling match. Dro's hurt ribs left him vulnerable as they slung each other across the living room, both men bleeding from busted lips.

When the front door opened, Twenty rushed in, surprised to see his niggas fighting. "You niggas chill! Break this shit up!" he yelled, jumping in the middle.

Tae and Dro teamed up long enough to throw Twenty out of the way before they went at it again. Twenty pulled the .357 automatic from his waist and fired a shot into the ceiling. That got their attention.

"Fuck you niggas fightin' for? Chill!"

Tae checked his bleeding lip, mugging Dro before turning to Twenty. "Dog, you just put a hole in my ceiling."

"Fuck that ceiling, nigga. Fuck you niggas fighting about?"

"Nigga mouth got too slick, so I put blood in it," Dro said.

"Fuck you, nigga. If yo' soft ass woulda showed this same heart at Monster house and killed them girls, I wouldn't be beating yo' ass."

"You know you can't fight, nigga. I was beatin' yo' ass before you grabbed me, weak-ass nigga."

Tae moved like he was about to rush Dro, but Twenty grabbed him. "You niggas chill, fam. We ain't on that. This fighting shit over. Whatever y'all problems, y'all gon' talk that shit out like family. We brothers."

"Soft-ass nigga ain't my brother," Tae mugged.

"Fuck you, nigga. You ain't my brother, either. Just gimme my shit so I can leave."

"I ain't givin' you shit, nigga. Fuck out my house before I treat you like a op'," Tae spat.

"Oh, you wanna go there, nigga? You wanna get on that?" Dro asked, hurt that Tae had crossed that line, but ready to go there to get his money.

"You niggas chill!" Twenty snapped. "Y'all ain't finna do shit. Dro, step outside for a minute. I'ma grab yo' cut and bring it to you."

"Nah, that nigga betta go get my shit now or I'ma turn the fuck up!" Dro mugged.

"Dro, I got you, brah," Twenty said, trying to calm the situation. "But I ain't finna let y'all fight no more. That shit dead. Wait in yo' car and I'ma bring it out."

Dro gave Tae a long mug before walking outside. He was sitting in the Charger for a couple minutes before Twenty came out with a plastic bag and hopped in the passenger seat.

"This yo' shit. It's all there. You niggas trippin', brah."

"Fuck that nigga!" Dro barked. "That nigga be on too much ho-ass shit, trynna treat me like I'm a bitch. So, I hit that nigga in his shit. Soft-ass nigga."

"I told you that nigga was hot, Dro. And you like our lil'lil' brother. That nigga talk shit to er'body."

"So what? That nigga ain't finna be treating me like I'm a bitch. I get down, too."

"This what y'all finna be on, for real? Outta all the shit we been through, y'all finna fall out over this?"

Dro was silent, thinking on Twenty's words. The Savages had been through a lot together. They were more than brothers. They had been through wars together. He didn't want to beef with Tae, but he wasn't about to be treated like a bitch. "I don't give a fuck, brah. It's on that nigga. He the one that got on some extra shit, talking 'bout treatin' me like a op'. that shit wasn't a hunnit."

"Yeah, that was some bullshit. I'ma holla at that nigga 'bout that shit. Take some time to chill. Relax and get high and getcho mind right. You got seventy-five bands. Focus on how you gon' spend it. I'ma hit you later. Stay dangerous."

"Already. Savage."

After leaving Tae's house, Dro went to check on his uncle. Crush came out of the house looking and smelling like last week.

"Hey, Nephew. Wasn't expecting to see you today. What up?"

"I'm good. Just wanted to holla at you and see if you needed something."

"Nah, I'm good. You did enough for me already. Look like you got something on your mind. What happened to your lip?"

"Come take a ride with me, Unc. Grab something to eat."

When they were in the car, Dro got the words off his chest. "I'm done. I'm getting out."

Crush did a double-take. "Seriously? You getting out of the robbery game?"

"Yeah. Lotta shit happened in the last couple days. Where you wanna eat at?"

"Don't matter. McDonald's or Burger King is cool. So, what happened to your lip?"

"Tae was talking shit, and we got it up. We moved on Monster, and the nigga got salty because I didn't kill Monster kids. I couldn't do no shorties, Unc."

Crush's eyes grew wide. "Y'all killed Monster?"

"His whole family. One of them niggas shot me, too. Hit me in the vest and cracked my ribs."

"So, that did it, huh? This was the one that made you hang it up?"

"Yeah. I reached my money goal, and I made a promise to Forever to get out."

"Damn, Nephew. You burned it up out here. I think you making the right choice. Might not be a bad thing to skip town for a little while. Everybody in the streets is gon' try to figure out who hit Monster."

"I might, depending on how everything plays out. I still gotta tell my niggas I'm out. They ain't gon' like it. But Forever said she will help me. Man, Unc, I think she the one."

"If the Savages are your real friends, they will understand you wanting to do something different with your life. A real friend will give you the advantage, not take advantage. And this Forever sounds special."

"She is. She like my guardian angel or something. Her phone call saved my life, no bullshit. I was about to walk in front of a shotgun, but her call made me pause. Got hit in the vest. Shit, when we first met, after she ran me over, I was lying on the ground –"

"Wait. You mean she ran you over with her car?"

"Yeah. It was an accident. I was trynna chase a big booty broad across the street and walked in front of her truck."

He laughed. "No shit?"

"When I was lying on the ground looking at her in them headlights, I swear she looked like an angel. Then she saved my life."

"Hell of a story, Nephew. Only thing I gotta say is do what's right for you. I'm happy you're about to do the right thing. I would hate to hear about you getting locked up for life or end up in a box like yo' daddy. You gotta keep the Patrick bloodline going strong."

Chapter 15

"I was just about to call you," Forever smiled.

"I know. I felt it. That's why I'm calling. What you doin'?"

"I'm having a drink."

Dro frowned. "Seriously? Liquor?"

"That's what kind of day it's been."

"Wanna talk about it?"

"Not over the phone. Can you come to me?"

"Yeah. I just left Mom's. Where you at?"

"At 414 on Water Street. You know it?"

"Yeah. I'm on my way."

It took him fifteen minutes to reach her. 414 was an upscale bar downtown. After a hug and kiss, Dro sat next to her at the bar and ordered a beer.

"Hey, Ruben. I'm so glad you came."

"You know I won't let you down. So, what got you tossing back drinks before sundown?"

"I talked to Ken," she sulked.

"The white dude Spencer told us about?"

"Yeah. Him. He is a jerk in real life. I wanted to know more about how my mom died, and turns out he was there when she gave birth. Said my grandparents disowned my mom when they found out she was pregnant with a black baby. Then, after I was born and my mother died, he didn't know what to do, so he left. Said he didn't want to raise a baby that wasn't his all alone."

Dro shook his head. "That's messed up. Bet he wasn't thinkin' 'bout that when he was poking yo' moms, was he?"

She cut her eyes at him.

"What? I'm keeping it real. If he was with her for the pregnancy, he should've taken some responsibility."

"I thought about it the same way. What's wrong with people? Do you see why I'm drinking?"

"Yeah. Listening to that story made me want something harder," he said, taking a sip of beer.

"Enough about me. How are you? Did you think about what I said about going back to school?"

"Yeah, a lil'lil' bit. Don't really know what I wanna do."

"What about trade school? Welding or a computer course?"

"I think you been thinking too much," he laughed.

"Well, excuse me for trying to live up to my end of the deal."

"Nah, it ain't like that. I just didn't expect things to happen so fast. I wanted to ease into the change, not dive in head-first."

"But going to school will keep you busy. Maybe get a part-time job, too."

"Whoa, whoa, whoa! Slow down, shorty. You movin' too fast. One thing at a time. I was actually thinking about opening my own business."

Her eyes lit up. "That is a good idea. What kind of business are you interested in?"

"I'm not sure. That's what you here for, right? I need you to help me figure it out."

"You ever thought about buying into a franchise? Open a fast food restaurant. I heard it costs around fifty thousand to open a Dunkin' Donuts. You said you already had thirty."

He smiled. "Turns out I got a lil'lil' more than that. But I have to find a way to clean it."

She frowned. "That's outta my league. I don't know how to clean money. You're on your own with that one. Just don't do anything crazy."

After kicking it at the bar a little longer, they left for their cars, walking hand-in-hand. "Why do you have to kick it with your friends tonight? Don't you want to kick it with your girl?"

He gave her a look. "So, you my girl now? We making this official?"

"Stop playing, Ruben. You know what I mean. I meant girlfriend." Her eyes grew wide when she realized what she said. "I didn't mean girlfriend like that. We're friends, and I'm a girl."

"Do friends hold hands and kiss? Do friends also sleep together?"

She paused to stare up at him. "What are you saying?"

"That I want you. I think you're special, and I want to be more than friends. I want you to be my girl."

She continued to stare at him. "If I say yes, will you come back to my house and not go out with your friends?"

"C'mon, Forever. My dude, Luna, is gettin' bail. This my day-one. I gotta be there when he get out. Don't make me choose."

She let go of his hand and walked away. "Well, I guess you don't want a girlfriend."

He grabbed her arm, spinning her around and wrapping her in a hug. "Don't be like that, baby. C'mon now. I'm about to leave the streets for good. I don't got too much longer to kick it with them. Just gimme one more night."

"Okay. So, what are you doing after you finish kicking with your friends?"

He pecked her on the lips. "I was hoping I could be doing you."

"Ruben!" she blushed, slapping him on the shoulder. "I'm not going to play second fiddle tonight, or ever. Just call me when you get home."

"So, that's how it is? If I don't pick you first, I can't have you at all?"

She smiled, loving the game. "Yep. I'm not mad about it, though. I'm showing you that I come first. Have fun with your friends. And don't get into trouble. And call me when you make it home."

He shook his head, wanting to be mad but knew he couldn't. "You bogus, but okay. I might get home late. Do you still want me to call?"

"Yes. I need to make sure you get home safe. You get shot too much."

"I know, right?" he laughed. "Okay. Let me taste those lips again to remind me why I should call you later."

***

Dro left the bar with thoughts of Forever on his mind. Damn, he had it bad. He liked everything about her. The way she walked, talked, laughed, smiled, said his name, everything. She embodied everything a good woman should be. Good looks, a nice body, morals, smart, and most importantly, she wanted him to succeed.

Thoughts of his boo were interrupted by the phone ringing. He didn't recognize the number on the screen. "Hello?"

"Where you at, nigga? Come get me!" Lunatic screamed.

"When the fuck you get out, nigga? Where you at?"

"I'm on some nice lady phone outside the county jail. Come get me, nigga."

"I'm on my way right now. I'm already downtown. Be there in, like, five minutes."

When the Charger pulled to the curb outside the county jail, Lunatic limped over and climbed in the passenger seat.

"My nigga!" he smiled, hugging Dro like they hadn't seen each other in years. "You betta have some weed, nigga!"

"Look in the ashtray. What's good, boy? I see that bullet didn't slow you down. Why you ain't have Whisper or somebody out here waiting on you?"

"'Cause I wanted to kick it wit' chu, nigga. And can't no bullets slow me down, nigga. I'm bulletproof," he laughed.

"I hear you. I been gettin' shot so much lately that I think I'm bulletproof, too. Caught a slug in my vest when we hit Monster that fucked me up."

"I wish I coulda been there when y'all offed his bitch-ass. Ho-ass nigga."

"Tae and Twenty got his bitch-ass. I was still lyin' on the floor."

"Speaking of Tae, I hard you niggas was scrapping. What that shit was about?"

"Nigga was talkin' shit 'cause I didn't off Monster daughters. I took off on that nigga."

Lunatic laughed. "You niggas crazy. Have you talked to him since?"

"Hell nah. Nigga got to talkin' 'bout treatin' me like a op. I'm really on some fuck-that-nigga-type shit."

"Nah, Dro. That ain't goin' down like that. You niggas gon' have to figure that shit out. We brothers."

"Yeah, I hear you. That's my nigga, but he was outta pocket. Where you trynna go? I know you wanna get in some new clothes."

"Right now I need you to stop at the liquor store so I can get some Yak. Then take me to the condo so I can get some pussy and a shower. You strapped?"

"You know I don't leave the house without my shit. It's in the glove box."

Luna grabbed it, keeping it on his lap. "Let me hold this bitch. Niggas on lock was sayin' we had somethin' to do wit' Monster gettin' knocked off. We gon' have to be on point. I think we might gotta price on our heads."

Dro glanced at him. "On what?"

"That's what niggas was sayin' in there. But you know I'm built to last. If they come for me, they betta have a army."

Dro became quiet, thinking about the price tag on his head. The streets was a bitch. A bloodthirsty, no good, punk-ass bitch. "I'm done with this shit, brah," he mumbled.

Lunatic chuckled. "You know what, Dro? The whole time I was on lock, I kept thinkin', 'What if I never see the streets again?' Outta all the shit we done, this was the first time it ever hit me like that. I almost got murked, my nigga. It's so much shit that I ain't did yet. I ain't trynna die before I'm thirty."

"I been thinking the same shit for a couple months. I got a daughter I need to live for."

"This why I called you to come get me. I can't talk to Tae or Twenty 'bout this shit. Them niggas eat gunpowder and shit bullets. I know you into Jesus and all that. I always respected that you ain't let what we do in the streets take that from you. I went to church a couple times while I was in the county. Prayed and er'thang."

Dro smiled. "That's what's up. Gotta have God on yo' side."

"Real talk, I knew you wasn't gon' be on that savage shit forever. You one of the smartest niggas I know. And you got a good family. If you ain't feelin' it no more, get out."

"Monster was my last move."

"You told Tae or Twenty?"

"Nah. Just you and Crush. Them niggas too cutthroat to understand. Streets all they know."

"On er'thang! Only niggas I know sleep in vests and shit," Luna laughed.

When Dro pulled up to the liquor store, Lunatic dashed inside to get a pint of Hennessey. "You ever felt like God was watching you?" Dro asked when he climbed back in the car.

"Nah, brah. You gettin' too deep for me."

"Not watching like we watch TV. More like watching over a nigga. I been gettin' into jams, but somehow I always get out. Even when I was dead-ass. With this last shit, I feel like I cheated death. How a shotgun slug don't go through my vest at point-blank? I feel like God been trynna get my attention for a minute. Like He uses people and situations to tell me something. I know I supposed to be dead or in jail, but He keep giving me chances. I don't know how many I got left, and I wanna get out while I still got the opportunity."

"Damn, Dro. That shit got me thinkin' 'bout my life, nigga. All the chances I done had. I think I'ma jump in the game wit' Whisper after I put this case behind me. Talked about moving to Atlanta. We gotta make it out this shit, Dro. Ain't no future in gettin' shot up or goin' to jail."

***

From the liquor store, Dro drove to The Ho Whisperer's condo. Ten bad bitches dressed in lingerie rushed Luna as soon as they walked in the door.

"Nephew! Welcome home, young nigga!" Whisper called, smiling like a proud father.

"What it do, Unc? This how a nigga s'posed to be welcomed home!" Luna grinned as the women led him to the bathroom.

"Young Dro, what's up with you, baby boy?" Whisper asked.

"Not too much. Pimpin'. But I do need a little advice on how to clean my money. I'm thinking 'bout opening a business."

Whisper looked at him like he was sick. "Where is Dro and what the fuck you do wit' my lil'lil' nigga?"

"C'mon, Whisper. I'm serious. I been thinkin' 'bout what you said. I think I need a change of hustle."

"You think?"

"I know. We got a nice chunk of change from Monster, and I wanna do something smart with it."

"'Bout time one of y'all started using ya head. I know somebody that will clean it for thirty percent. Take him a hunnit Gs and he'll give you back a clean seventy."

"Damn, man," Dro frowned. "That's kinda expensive."

"That's how it works in the real world, youngin'. But it's worth it. Can't do nothing with dirty money or the feds gon' bust yo' ass and take it all."

Dro let out a long breath, not liking the thought of losing thirty grand. "Can you give me his number?"

"I got you, Young Dro. Matter fact, I'll make the call for you tomorrow. He outta the country right now. Just call me tomorrow."

Dro and Whisper sat back, smoking blunts and kicking it when there was a knock on the front door/ "I'll get it," one of the women called.

A few moments later Twenty walked in the living room. Tae was close behind, a small, dark bruise under his right eye.

"Dro, Whisper, What it do? Where my nigga at?" Twenty asked, looking around for Lunatic.

"He in the bathroom gettin' fluffed and pampered. Have a seat. Smoke with us."

Tae walked in front of Dro and stopped. "Quit trynna look hard, nigga, and show me some love," he grinned.

"What up, nigga?" Dro chuckled, standing to embrace his brother in arms.

"I know you didn't think that shit was gon' break up the squad. We family, lil'lil' nigga."

"You know it's all love," Dro nodded.

Whisper watched Dro and Tae, not in the loop on the make-up. "What's goin' on with y'all? Something happen I don't know about?"

"Them niggas was on some Kane and Abel shit the other day," Twenty cracked.

Whisper's eyes grew wide. "Oh, yeah? That's why you got that dot under yo' eye, huh, Tae? I know who won!" he laughed.

"Hell nah," Tae frowned, touching the bruise. "Nigga snuck me when I wasn't looking."

Dro burst out laughing. "You jackin', brah. You know these hands work."

"Fuck you, nigga. We can go again."

"Now, hold on! Y'all ain't about to be fighting up in here," Whisper warned. "Besides, I need to talk to y'all about some serious shit. Sit down Tae."

"What you talkin' 'bout, pimpin'?" Twenty asked, plopping down on the couch.

"I think it might be some numbers on y'all heads. I'm not a hunnit percent sure, but it's some rumblings in the streets. They sayin' y'all knocked off Monster."

Tae laughed. "That shit crazy, brah."

"Who supposed to be puttin' up the check?" Twenty asked.

"I'm not sure. That's why I said I'm not a hunnit percent. Right now it's just a rumor. I'm lettin' y'all know so you won't get caught slipping. After all, most rumors got a level of truth to them."

Twenty patted the pistol on his waist. "Tell them bitches to come get me."

"I got a Draco outside that can't wait to bust a nut," Tae added.

After kicking it at the condo, the party went to the strip club, and the whole hood showed up to welcome Lunatic home.

"Shit crazy, Dro," Nu-Nu mumbled, looking around the club suspiciously. "How you niggas got numbers on y'all heads, but still out here partying? Ain't this how Luna got popped?"

"Hell, yeah," Dro nodded, throwing a handful of singles on the stage as he watched the strippers put on a show. "But you know we ain't duckin' shit. Niggas gon' have to bring it. Hold my spot. I'm finna hit the bar and get anotha bottle."

Nu-Nu's words played in Dro's mind as he made his way to the bar. For the hundredth time he asked himself what the fuck he was doing in the club fronting like they didn't have a care in the world. He knew better. But the rest of his niggas didn't. So here they were.

"Young Dro!" Lunatic called.

He looked over and seen his nigga getting a lap dance from two strippers. "I see you, nigga!"

"I'm leavin' wit' both of 'em!" Lunatic laughed, slapping them on the asses

After giving a nod, Dro continued to the bar. He was a few feet away when his Spidey Sense began tingling. Instead of looking around to see who was watching him, he walked up to the bar and ordered a bottle of Moet. A fine and thick light-skinned woman stood next to him, also ordering drinks.

"'Sup with you, ma?" he asked.

She spun to give him a quick head-to-toe. "In here turning up!" she smiled.

"That's what's up. Me too," he said, casually turning around to look out over the club. "I'm Dro. What's yo' name?"

"Hey, Dro. I'm Mashonda. What y'all celebrating?"

He was about to respond when he spotted the cause of his tingling Spidey Sense. A dark-skinned nigga with bug-like eyes and a long scar across the right side of his face was watching him. After locking eyes, the man looked away.

"Thanks for the good conversation," Mashonda said with a little attitude before grabbing her drink and walking away.

Dro ignored her, trying to remember why the nigga with the scar on his face made him feel some type of way. He looked familiar, but Dro wasn't sure why. And then the nigga seemed to disappear in the club.

He went to find Twenty. "Brah, you remember a black-as-ass nigga wit' fish eyes and a long scar on his face?"

He thought for a moment. "Nah, I don't think so. Why?"

"Nigga was watchin' me at the bar. Now I can't find the nigga."

"Could be anybody. Or you just paranoid about them prices on our heads. But I'ma keep my eyes open."

"Why y'all over here lookin' all serious?" s stripper asked, sitting on Dro's lap.

"I was waiting on somebody to come over here and give me a reason to relax."

***

Dro awoke the next morning to his bladder giving him a hard time. As he stumbled to the bathroom, he noticed he was still fully-dressed, mouth drier than a desert tomb. While he took a piss long enough to set a world record, he thought about the previous night. Everything was foggy, and he wasn't sure how he got home. He remembered entering the strip club, and not much after that.

After going to the kitchen to quench his thirst, he grabbed the phone to check messages. Forever left a voicemail an hour ago.

"Hey, Ruben. I got your message this morning. Thanks for calling. You're so sweet. And you sounded wasted. Reminded me of my college days. You probably don't even remember what you said," she laughed. "I have to get back to work. Call me when you wake up."

He tried calling her, but she didn't answer. Next he called The Ho Whisperer.

"What's up, Dro?"

"You got it, pimpin'. I'm calling to remind you to call yo' money man."

"Oh, shit. I forgot about that. I'ma call him right now. I'ma give him yo' number. Now, don't be on no bullshit, lil'lil' nigga. He a legit businessman."

"I'm not on bullshit, Whisper. I'm serious about gettin' my shit together. I'm tired of the drama."

"Sounds like you growing up and getting wiser. Ain't no sense risking yo' life for some money if you don't live long enough to spend it. I'ma make that call. Hold yo' head."

After spending most of the day in the house, Dro hit the mall to buy a new outfit and pick out something for Forever. They were meeting at a restaurant after she got off work, and he wanted to do something nice.

***

"Hey, baby!" Forever smiled, puckering up for a kiss.

"Hey, you. How was your day? Hungry?"

"I'm so hungry I could eat two full course meals by myself. I'm starved," she said, picking up her menu. "What did you do today? You look surprisingly well for somebody that called me sloppy-drunk and four o'clock in the morning."

"Was it that late? What did I say?"

The smile on her face let him know he said something he would regret. "Oh my God! I'm keeping this voicemail forever. Listen," she said, pulling out her phone and playing the message.

"Forever. Hey, baby. Shit. Uh. Yeah. I just got in the house, and I was thinkin' 'bout chu all night. I started to come over, but I forgot where you lived. Ha ha! Damn. I'm fucked up. Oops. Sorry for cussin'. I just wanted to let you know that I'm feelin' you, for real, for real. I-I-I wanna grow old wit' chu, girl. I was listening to that song by Keyshia Cole. You remember this? '*Love! Never knew what I was missin'. But I knew –*'"

Dro reached for the phone. "Okay. I get it. You gotta erase that message."

She snatched the phone away. "Nope. I'm keeping this. I'm going to play it when we get old," she laughed.

"That's how you gon' do me?"

"It's cute, Ruben. One day you'll laugh at this."

"Yeah, whatever. Guess what I did today?"

"Not much since you were probably hung over," she laughed.

"I talked to a guy about cleaning my money. He's going to help me open a couple laundromats."

She dropped the menu, eyes watering like she wanted to cry. "Oh, Ruben! I'm so proud of you. I knew you could do it."

"I got something for you, too," he said, pulling a jewelry box from his pocket and sliding it across the table.

Her eyes grew wide as the sun. "Oh, my God! What is this?"

"Open it."

Inside was a diamond-studded, rose gold heart pendant on an 18" rose gold chain.

"Oh, my God! It's beautiful!"

He stood and put it around her neck. "I was thinking about you while I was in the mall. Glad you like it."

When he sat back down, Forever stared at him, unable to wipe the smile from her lips. "When I first met you, I didn't like you. Now?" She shook her head, sighing. "I was mad at you when you quoted that scripture. Really, really mad. Then, the next day, that same scripture was in my daily devotional. I saved it in my phone. You've opened my eyes in so many ways. You've shown me there is more to a person than what we see on the outside. When you told me your name was Dro and you just got out of jail, I wanted to be as far away from you as possible. But now, I never want to leave your side. A couple weeks ago I went out with this guy, Calvin –"

"You went on a date with somebody?" Dro asked, feeling some type of way.

Excitement flashed in her eyes. "Are you jealous?"

"Quit playin', girl. I just remember you clearly saying you didn't date."

162

"Well, it wasn't a date, per say. I was doing Sasha a favor. She was going out with this guy and needed a wing woman."

"So, not only was it a date, but a double date."

"Ruben, it wasn't like that. Just let me finish. Anyway, when I met Calvin, he seemed like the kind of guy I would be interested in. He is a Christian rapper, has a job, and goes to school. But the entire time I was out with him, I compared him to you. And then he got a couple drinks in him and turned into a different person. Got freaky and disrespectful."

"A wolf in sheep's clothing," Dro laughed.

"And then some. But that situation and everything that's happened since we met makes me feel like we were supposed to meet."

"You was supposed to run me over?" he questioned.

"Stop playing. Well, maybe, because I don't believe in coincidences. I think we're connected."

Dro became serious. "I've been thinking the same thing, Forever. Real talk. Especially the night...."

"What were you about to say? Why did you stop?"

A gleam shown in his eyes. "You ever feel like God was trying to tell you something? Not literally talking, but using people and situation."

"Yes. That's how God works."

"That's been happening to me for as long as I can remember. Giving me all kinds of chances, you know? Warning me before I do things or helping me out of situations I shouldn't have gotten out of. Even when the odds get stacked against me, I always get out of the jam. Then, in this last situation, a text from you literally saved my life. I was about to walk into a room, and somebody was waiting on the other side of the door with a shotgun. When my phone vibrated, I paused, and that saved me. That's how I got shot in my vest. If I woulda took another step, I wouldn't be sitting at this table with you right now. I think you my guardian angel."

Forever looked blown away. "Wow, Ruben! I don't know what to say. That's an amazing story."

"I think we said it all. You know what this means, right?"

Her eyebrows furrowed. "What?"

"Means you stuck with me. You saved me, and I'm all yours."

She smiled, touching the heart pendant. "That might not be a bad thing."

Chapter 16

"Hey, Daddy!" Forever smiled, FaceTiming with her father.

"Daddy. Wow. That's going to take some getting used to," Spencer laughed. "What are you up to?"

"Nothing. Over here being ignored by Ruben."

"I'm not ignoring her, Spence. I'm watching a movie," Dro spoke up.

"Whatever. Watch your stupid movie about flying people that shoot electricity out of hammers. I have another man in my life."

Dro gave her a look before turning his attention back to the Avengers movie.

"I'm thinking about coming to Wisconsin next week to hang out with you. Can you make some time in your busy life to kick it with your old man?"

"I would love it if you came. You can stay at my apartment."

"Yeah. I'm thinking about next weekend. I have some sick days that I need to use."

"That would be great. I can't wait. I've been on my own for so long that it'll be fun having you around."

"Well, you're not alone anymore, baby girl. I know it's only been a couple of weeks since we got the results back, but I love you like I've known you for your whole life. And I will always be here for you."

"Aw, thanks, Dad."

"No problem, baby. Hey, I gotta finish up a run for Marty. I get off work in an hour. Can I call you back when I get home?"

"That's fine. I just wanted somebody to show me some attention for a few minutes. Call me when you get home."

"So, that's how it is?" Dro chuckled. "I don't show you no attention?"

"Not now. You're watching the stupid movie."

"This what I do since I ain't been in the hood. You would rather have me here with you watching movies than out with the Savages, right?"

She rolled her eyes. "Whatever. So, how are you doing now that you haven't been hanging with your boys so much anymore?"

"I'm smoking more weed than I used to."

"That's not a good thing."

"At least I'm being real. Everything won't happen overnight. I ain't no light switch. When I get bored, I smoke. But I'm kind of getting the hang of going to church again, even though I feel like the biggest sinner in the building."

"No sin is bigger than another."

"Yeah? Tell that to God for me. Now, can I get back to the movie?"

She stared at him for a moment to see if he was serious. He was. "I hate you."

Dro smiled before stretching out on the couch, his head in her lap, and got back to the movie. Forever rubbed his waves and looked at the TV, but wasn't watching the movie. Instead she was thinking about her Ruben. They had been inseparable since coming back from North Dakota. When she wasn't at work, they were together. Feelings were being developed, and she felt it was time to have the conversation.

"How do you feel about me, Ruben?"

He turned to look up at her. "What?"

"Ever since we've come back from meeting my father, we haven't left each other's side. I want to know how you feel about it."

Dro gave his undivided attention. "I think you already know how I feel. I like being around you. I like who I am when I'm with you. You make me better. And I don't want you to go nowhere. Now, tell me how you feel about me."

"I could repeat everything you just said. You make me a better woman. And I'm not going anywhere. I'm here to stay."

Dro smiled. "So, can we stop playing games and make it official? I'm yo' man and you my woman, right?"

Her eyes lit up. "Right."

"Seal it with a kiss."

She leaned forward to kiss him, a question lighting her eyes when she sat back up.

"What?" he asked.

"Nothing."

"I know you, Forever. You got that look in your eyes. What?"

"Well, um. How do you like the way we make love?"

The question surprised him. "We good. You good. Why you ask me that?"

"Because I haven't slept with that many people, so I'm inexperienced. And you're way better than my ex-boyfriend. He said I wasn't outgoing enough in bed."

Dro laughed. "What does that even mean? And how many people have you been with?"

"I don't know what he meant by that. And I've only been with one man. Consensually."

His face showed disbelief. "Only one person? For real?"

"Yes. What's your number?"

He looked away. "I don't know. Never really counted."

"Stop playing," she laughed. "All men keep count. Ballpark estimate?"

"Somewhere between fifty and a hundred."

Her eyes bucked. "Oh my God, Ruben! You're a whore!" she scoffed

"You wanted me to lie?"

"No. But that's a lot. Geesh."

"Well, you asked. So, who was this dude you slept with? Tell me about him."

"His name is Steven. We met in college."

He looked at her expectantly. "That's all you gotta say?"

"What else do you want to know?"

"What happened? Why did y'all break up? Were you in love?"

"Of course I loved him. He was my first boyfriend. I fell hard and fast. I was naïve, so I believed everything he told me. Even when I didn't see him for days and weeks, I believed the lies he told. No questions asked. Whenever I asked too many questions, he got upset and disappeared. So I stopped everything and just believed what he said. That went on for two years. Then I was out buying a new couch one day and ran into him at the store. But he wasn't alone. He was with a guy dressed like a woman. Turned out Steven was gay and was with his boyfriend for five years. I was the side chick."

Dro looked blown away. "Damn, Forever. You've been through some shit, baby."

"Yeah. I know how to pick them, right?" she joked. "Went from a gay man to a robber."

"Ex-robber," he clarified.

"Yeah. An ex-robber that smokes too much weed."

"Which really ain't a big deal because it's about to be legal all over for recreational use. It'll be just like having a beer or glass of wine."

***

The first thing Dro noticed when he awoke was the absence of her presence. Whenever Forever was around, he could feel her. Like they shared the same heartbeat. That's how he knew she wasn't in another part of the house. And even though he knew she was gone, he still reached out to feel her side of the bed. Empty.

When he finally opened his eyes, he sat up to look around. All traces of Forever were gone, and he didn't even hear her leave. After reaching for the phone, he checked the time. 8:14 a.m. He thought about what he should do for the day. Nothing came to mind. Not being in the streets left him with a lot of down time. He had been thinking about getting a job until he finalized the plans for the laundromats, but thinking about it was as far as he got.

The vibrating of the phone pulled him from further thoughts. It was his mother. "G'morning, Mama."

"Good morning, Ruben. How are you doing?"

"I'm cool. Just woke up."

"Good. I'm glad you're awake. I wanted to talk to you."

"C'mon, Mama. You know you can't lead off a conversation like that and expect a man to be interested."

"Good thing the man is my son," she laughed. "I'm happy you're getting your life together, and I want to be there to help you. To support you. Me and Lenny are so proud of you."

"Thanks, Moms. Trynna walk the straight and narrow feels kinda crazy."

"Nothing worth having will come easy. So, how are those plans to start your own business coming?"

"Good. I have to choose a sight and buy the equipment. I got a meeting in a couple days."

"Hallelujah! Praise God! God is good."

"Yes, He is."

"That's right, son. I thank God all the time for answering our prayers for you. I'm so happy I get to witness this miracle."

"Yeah. The prodigal son found his way home," he laughed.

"I know that's right. So, when do I get to meet this Forever? I'm so anxious to meet the woman that got my son to stop running the streets."

"Um, I don't know," he stalled.

"Well, you know I was thinking about making chicken dumplings tonight."

That made Dro's mouth water and stomach growl. "Chicken dumplings? Why you gotta think about that? Just make 'em."

"Yeah, that and I just got a recipe from Sister James for a roasted pineapple and brown sugar coconut ice cream gingersnap crumble."

"I don't even know what that is, but it sound good. Go 'head and put that together. I'ma be over later."

"You plus one, right?"

He laughed. "Okay. You got me. I'ma talk to her after she get off work. But y'all bet not be on no mess like y'all was when I brought America over for the first time."

His mother let out a hearty laugh. "America was a mess, son. Came in here with no tact and acting all ghetto. She needed Jesus. But I love my grandbaby. Y'all got that right."

"They like night and day, Mom. But y'all still betta be on y'all best behavior."

"We will. Okay, son. I'ma start getting this food ready. See you later."

"A'ight, Ma. Bye."

After hanging up the phone, he went to shower, wondering how he would tell Forever his mother wanted to meet. Tonight. One thing was for sure, she would be surprised to hear the news.

When he came out of the bathroom, he seen a missed call from America.

"What up? You called?"

"Yeah. Where you at?"

"At home. Why?"

"Um, because I wanna talk."

He felt the same twitch in his gut when his mom said those words. "A'ight. Talk. Somethin' wrong with Asia?"

"Nah, she at school. She good. But I don't want to talk over the phone. It's important, and we need to talk in person. Can you come over?"

All kinds of thoughts ran through his mind as he tried to think of what she could want. She must've heard something in the streets. "A'ight. Let me get dressed. I'm on my way."

***

Forty-five minutes later he parked behind America's Camry. When he knocked on the door, America answered quickly, looking way too happy to see him.

"Hey, baby daddy!" she smiled. "Come in."

He looked her over as he stepped in the house. She wore light make-up and a skin-tight, red body suit that left nothing to the imagination. His baby mama was beyond strapped. "Where you goin' with that on?"

"Nowhere. I put this on for you."

He stopped in the middle of the living room. "What you on, ma?"

She cocked her head to the side and put a hand on one of those crazy-wide hips. "Really, nigga? You gotta ask? Me and Chris ain't working out. He cool, but he ain't you. The only reason I stayed with him was to make you jealous, but that didn't work. Since you won't make the first move, I will."

Dro was about to protest, but America became aggressive, pushing him on the couch and climbing on top. She dry-humped his lap and stuck her tongue down his throat.

Dro got with the program, palming her phatty, dick harder than a steel beam.

"Yeah, baby! Shh! Suck these," she purred, pulling down the front of the cat suit, exposing those Double-Ds. Dro popped a nipple in his mouth and sucked on it like he was breastfeeding.

"Mm! Yeah, baby," she moaned, rubbing his head.

Dro had just popped the other nipple in his mouth when she pushed his head back roughly, bending to kiss him. Her hands moved to his pants, undoing the button and releasing his meat. "You missed me, didn't you?" she asked, snaking her way down his body.

He didn't miss her, but he definitely missed her head. Forever hadn't even attempted to suck his dick yet, and just thinking about what America could do with her lips had him super excited.

"Oh, shit! Damn, girl!" he moaned when she took him all the way down her throat. She bobbed her head up and down a few times before placing a kiss on the head. "I'm so glad you came over, baby. I got a surprise that you gon' love."

"A'ight. Tell me later," he said, trying to push her head back to his dick.

"Wait. Don't you wanna see my surprise?" she asked, some kind of mischief flashing in her eyes.

"A'ight. What is it?"

She got up from her knees wearing a smile. "Be right back. Don't you move."

As soon as America left the room, thoughts of Forever jumped into Dro's head. They were less than a month in and he was about to cheat. The temptation proved too much. He thought about getting up and leaving, attempting to keep some integrity intact. But when he looked down at his dick pointing in the air like a sword, he knew he wasn't going to be able to leave until they finished what America started.

"Dro! Here I come," America called before popping back in the living room naked. And she wasn't alone.

"Hey, Dro," Shamika smiled. She was also naked and eyeing his hard tool like it was a delicious piece of candy.

He looked at both of the naked women before him, feeling his dick grow harder. Like America, Shamika was strapped: light-skinned, blonde hair cut low like Amber Rose, big-ass titties, small waist, wide hips, pussy shaved, and an ass so big it clapped when she walked.

"'Sup, Shamika?" Dro nodded, checking out her body.

"America said she needed some help. Now I see why."

"Why you still got yo' clothes on?" his baby momma asked.

Dro stood and ripped his clothes off like it was an NBA warm-up suit. When he sat back on the couch, the women sat on either side, kissing and licking his chest and neck. America's hand found his dick, and Shamika's found his balls. The anticipation of the threesome had Dro so geeked up that he busted, shooting onto his stomach and the women's hands.

"Damn! You really did miss me," America said before bending and licking nut from his stomach.

Shamika joined in, helping to lick him clean before they took turns giving him head and sucking his balls. The second nut erupted in Shamika's mouth, and she swallowed it all. And he was still hard.

"G'on, get you some of that," America encouraged her friend.

The thicker-than-a-Snickers vixen's booty clapped as she stood and prepared to ride him reverse cowgirl. For no other reason than to feel her ass, Dro gripped her cheeks and spread them apart as she eased down on him.

"Damn, Dro!" Shamika moaned as she worked her hips.

"Yeah, baby. Work that shit," Dro groaned, loving how tight and wet her pussy felt. He watched her big-ass booty jiggle and bounce as she rode him faster. A few moments later there was wetness around his balls as America began sucking them. When his baby mama's mouth disappeared, Shamika let out a sharp cry.

"Shh! Oh, shit! Damn, girl!"

Dro leaned to the side and seen America sucking her friend's clit while she rode him. That shit was sexy as fuck, and he couldn't take his eyes off the action.

"Oh, shit! Oh, shit!" Shamika cried as her body began jerking and her walls tightened around his pole. Then she sat all the way down and came, wetting his lap.

"Damn," Shamika panted. "That shit felt good as fuck."

"Good. Now get yo' ass up. It's my turn," America said as she stood.

When Shamika stood, they did some erotic kissing before America pulled Dro in to share the three-way kiss. Then the threesome went to the floor. America was on her back, legs in the air, Dro deep in her guts while Shamika sat on her face, riding America's tongue like it was a vibrator turned on high.

An hour later they were lying in America's bed, smoking a blunt.

"How many times y'all did this before, and how long I been missing out?" Dro asked.

"First threesome we ever had," Shamika said.

"But we been messing around for years. Nothing serious. When you used to be gone for too long, sometimes she scratched my itch," America explained.

Dro felt left out. "So, we coulda been gettin' it on all this time? Y'all been holding out?"

"It wasn't like that, Dro. For real. We just fucked around every now and then. Plus, I was with Jeff."

"And her and Jeff broke up a couple weeks ago," America added. "She been staying here for a couple days. But if you want, it could be permanent."

The offer made Dro pause and think. He had been presented with the opportunity to live every nigga's fantasy. The chance to come home to two bad bitches every night was tempting as hell. But what about Forever? He hadn't thought of her since Shamika and America walked out of the room naked, but now that she was in his head, he couldn't get her out. And the guilt of cheating on her came back, too.

"Where you at, nigga?" Shamika asked, pulling him from the guilt trip.

"I'm here," he said, passing her the blunt. "Take this."

"So, when you want me to kick Chris square ass to the curb? When you coming back?" America asked, knowing she got her nigga.

"I can't do it, baby," he mumbled.

Both women gave sharp looks, eyeing him like he was crazy. "Why not? You can have two bad bitches, nigga. Fuck is in this weed?" Shamika asked.

Dro tried to think of the words to say.

America rolled on top of Dro to look him in the face. "What's up? Why you not talking? Did you meet another bitch?"

"Yeah," he breathed.

"And she badder than us?" Shamika asked incredulously, not believing he could do better than the two of them.

Dro took a moment to consider her words. America and Shamika were bad bitches indeed, but the truth was Forever was badder. And even though America once had his heart and would always occupy a small part of it, the rest of it belonged to Forever.

"Listen, America. You know you my girl, and you gon' always be. And this threesome was the shit! Had this happened a couple months ago, I would be in. But I met somebody, and I'm really feeling her."

America hissed like an eighteen-wheeler's air brake. "So, we done? For real?"

"I'ma always love you, baby. But like I told you before, we make better friends."

She got mad. "Why you didn't tell me this shit before we fucked? Damn, nigga."

"Because I missed yo' ass. And you answered the door looking all good in that cat suit, and a nigga couldn't resist. I coulda lied and made up some shit, but I love and respect you too much to do you like that. I'm keeping it real 'cause I don't want nothing to come between us."

America went quiet. Shamika turned up. "So, who is the bitch? What's her name? What do she look like to have yo' playa-for-life-ass whipped."

"Her name Forever. And she good."

"Good as in looks, or a good girl?"

"Both."

Shamika shook her head. "That's crazy. Yo' thugged-out ass got turned out by a good girl. Damn, America. Forever puttin' us bad bitches on notice."

Even though the situation wasn't funny, Dro laughed at her comment.

"So, if I got a itch, will you come scratch it?" America asked.

"Probably not. I'ma try to do the right thing. I'm going legit and getting out the streets. Opening my own business."

America's eyes popped. "Say what now?"

"Yeah. I been thinkin' 'bout doin' this for a while. I wanna be around for Asia."

Knowing another woman got Dro to do what she had always wanted him to do was crushing America's heart, bringing her to the verge of tears. "Damn, Dro. I'm hurt, and I swear I wanna be mad, but I can't. Sound like she must be a good woman, because you making changes I never thought you would. She gotta be a better woman than me to make you straighten up. But I'm happy you trynna do the right thing. Asia need you around. I appreciate you keeping it real. It's hard for me to accept, but I will. Eventually."

The bedroom went quiet for a few moments.

"And I want her to meet Asia."

"Oh, hell nah!" Shamika mugged.

Some kind of darkness clouded America's eyes.

"I ain't gon' do you how you did me with Chris. At least I'm lettin' 'you know."

America smirked. "You got me on that. I was wrong for sneaking her around Chris. They can meet. But don't think that bitch gon' replace me."

177

"Stop playing, baby. You know you one in a million."

Shamika reached down and grabbed Dro's dick. "Well, since this probably the last time we fuck, let's make it count."

***

Dro left America's house regretting giving up the two-for-one package, but knowing Forever was worth it. And he swore he would never cheat on her again, no matter what. No matter how hard things got, he would give Forever his all. She deserved it.

After driving a couple of blocks, his phone began vibrating. It was Tae. "What it do?"

"Dro, what up, nigga? Where you at?"

"I ain't on shit. Just left America's house."

"Still on that daddy dearest shit, huh, nigga?" Tae cracked.

"Fuck you, nigga," Dro laughed. "But I'm on that. Gotta make time for my girl."

"Asia or America?"

"That's why you called? To see what I be doing with my girls?"

"Nah, nigga. I'm just fucking with you. I called to see what you on. Niggas on Garfield posted. Ain't seen you in a minute, and we wanna know what up wit' our nigga. We Savages."

Dro didn't really want to go on Garfield. Nothing good happened in the hood. He really wanted to tell him he was done with the game, but that wasn't a conversation to have over the phone. "Shit, I was just heading that way right now."

"On what? That's what's up. Come holla at yo' boyz. Stay dangerous."

"You already know. Savage."

As soon as he hung up the phone, Dro got a strange feeling in his gut. Like something bad was about to happen. Either that or it was some kind of guilt for going to the hood after promising Forever he wouldn't. But he needed to holla at his niggas about the decision to leave the squad. So he ignored the gut feeling and drove on.

When he turned onto 42nd Street, the block was alive with all kinds of activity. Cars on chrome, music blasting, kids running around, and niggas standing in groups on the sidewalks and porches. Nu-Nu's porch was filled with niggas from the hood and the Savages.

"Young Dro!" Nu-Nu called when he stepped from the Charger.

"What's good, fam? 'Sup wit' chu niggas?" Dro greeted.

"Shit. Posted," Twenty grinned, his eyes low and red. "You ain't been in the hood in a minute. What up?"

"I been spending time with the fam. Asia an' 'em been keeping me busy. Plus, I'm trynna start a business. My money gon' make me some money."

"That's what's up," Lunatic nodded. "I was just tellin' niggas that I'm gettin' the fuck outta Milwaukee when I put this case behind me. I'm hittin' Atlanta with Whisper. 'Bout to do it real big!"

"Hell yeah!" Trouble nodded. "Tell that nigga to put my name in the hat if he need a shooter."

"Me, too," Nu-Nu added.

Dro seen that Lunatic had given him a way to break the news, and he took it. "I been thinking about –"

"Who the fuck is that?" Tae cut him off."

Everyone turned as a black, old school Cutlass inched down the block slowly.

"Y'all know who that is?" Twenty asked, going for his waist.

Before anybody could answer, automatic handguns flew out the front and rear passenger windows and shots rang out. Twenty, Tae, and Lunatic pulled out heat and shot back. The block was turned into a war zone. There were screams as people ran and ducked, trying to get out of the way of the hot lead. Dro lay on the ground, watching the Savages stand on the porch and exchange shots with the niggas in the car.

Then the Cutlass engine revved and the car sped away. Twenty ran off the porch and kept shooting at the car until it turned the corner. Then the block went quiet.

The aftermath was bloody. Two bodies lay on the sidewalk. Trouble was screaming in pain, and Rich Boy wasn't moving. Day-Day lay on the porch steps, writhing in pain.

Having seen enough, Dro ran to his Charger and seen bullet holes in the door and back window. He pulled away, wondering how many chances he had left.

Chapter 17

"How do I look?" Forever asked, twirling in a circle.

"For the millionth time, you good, baby," Dro breathed. He was sitting on her bed, judging her third change of clothes. They were supposed to be heading to his mother's house so she could meet the family, but Forever was stuck deciding what to wear.

"You don't think these jeans make my butt stick out too much?" she asked, lifting the dinner jacket to show her round backside.

Dro got stuck admiring her ass. When he didn't respond, she looked back and caught him staring. "Ruben!"

He jumped like she scared him. "What? Nah, you good. Everything is good," he said before getting up and wrapping her in his arms. "Don't worry about yo' clothes. Remember what the Bible say about not worrying what we will eat, drink, or wear. This one of those moments. Stop trippin'. You look good in whatever you wear. You so bad you could get away with rocking a trash bag. You good, baby. Trust me."

She melted on the inside, reaching up to kiss him. "Thank you, baby. You always know what to say."

"Now, is we done? 'Cause if we don't get up outta here, we gon' miss the start of dinner. And if I miss out on my chicken dumplings —"

"Okay. I'm ready. Let me grab my purse."

When they walked outside, Forever frowned at the sight of the Corvette. "Why did you drive this? Where is your other car?"

Dro stiffened. "Oh, um, I had to put it in the shop. It wouldn't start this morning."

She peered over the roof at him, knowing he lied. Since it wasn't a big deal, she didn't bother questioning him about it.

Twenty minutes later they pulled up to the family house and Forever got the jitters. "Oh, my God! I'm so nervous."

"They won't bite, baby," Dro laughed. "You good. C'mon."

"Wait," she stalled. "How does my hair look?"

He put a hand on her thigh and squeezed. "Baby, chill. It's alright. Everything is fine. Yo' hair fine. Yo' clothes fine. You fine. Now, let's go."

After saying what he needed to say, he got out of the car, walked around to her side, and opened the door. Forever took several deep breaths before allowing him to help her out of the car.

They were almost to the porch when the neighbor came outside to check her mailbox. "Hi, Ruben. I haven't seen you in a while."

Dro smiled and waved at the older white lady. "Hey, Mrs. Booker. I've been busy. Stopping by tonight to introduce the family to my girlfriend. This is Forever."

"Hi, Forever. That is a really pretty name. Fits you."

"Hi, Mrs. Booker. Thank you for the compliment," Forever smiled.

"You're welcome. Ruben, tell Marcia I'll be over later with my plate," she joked.

"Will do. It was good seeing you."

"That was so polite," Forever smiled at Dro. "I bet she would be surprised if she knew you used to rob people."

"She know how I do. She was my getaway driver on a couple of moves."

Forever looked startled.

Dro laughed. "I'm just playing. But that woulda been funny, wouldn't it?"

When they walked in the house, Dro led the way into the living room. There was a teenager sitting on the couch, face in a cell phone. When she seen Dro, her face lit up.

"Hey, big brother."

"'Sup, bugger bear?" he asked, reaching out to hug her.

"C'mon, now. I'm getting too old for that, Rupaul."

"No, you ain't. Say hi to Forever."

"I will, as soon as you let me go," she said before extending a hand to Forever. "Hi. I'm Kailah."

"Hi, Kailah. It's nice to meet you."

"You, too. Can you cook? You look too pretty to be in the kitchen."

"Chill, bugger bear. Leave her alone. Where er'body at?"

"I was just trying to get to know her. Dang. Mommy and Shanice in the kitchen. Daddy somewhere in the house."

"You got all night to get to know her," Dro said, walking toward the back of the house.

"It's okay, Kailah. I know you meant well," Forever said. "Your brother doesn't understand women."

"Boys are stupid. I think they really are from Mars."

"C'mon, Forever," Dro called. "Come meet the rest of the family."

"Your little sister is too much," she laughed.

"You don't even know the half. She fourteen going on thirty-five."

"What does she know about Rupaul and boys being from Mars?"

"Kailah was one of the smartest little kids growing up. Started reading when she was two. She know everything about everything."

Forever looked surprised. "Wow. She is way too much."

"Ya boy is back!" Dro called when he walked in the kitchen.

His mother was bent over the stove, pulling a dessert out of the oven. Marcia was a pretty, brow-skinned woman in her mid-forties. She stood at an average height, hair flowing in big curls that draped past her shoulders. She wore an apron wrapped tightly around her full figure. Next to her was another teenager who looked like a spitting image of her mother, except she was light-skinned with an athletic build.

"Hey, baby!" Marcia crooned, floating over to give him a hug. Then she turned to Forever. "My goodness, you are beautiful. I'm Marcia. It is so nice to finally meet you."

"Thank you," Forever beamed, holding out a hand to shake. "It's nice to meet you, Mrs. Williams. Your food smells good."

"Oh no, sweetie. Call me Marcia. And we hug in this house," she said before wrapping Forever in a motherly embrace. "This is my daughter, Shanice. Did you meet the other one?"

"Yeah. Kailah is cool. Hi, Shanice."

"Hey, Forever," she waved. "It's nice to meet the girl who stopped my brother from being stupid."

"I ain't stupid, lil'lil' buster. And you wasn't saying that when you wanted them J's. Betcha I won't buy you nothing else."

"I didn't do anything, really. It was all God," Forever said humbly.

"No, honey. You played a big part in it," Marcia cut in. "Ruben, or Young Dro, as his friends call him, been stupid for a long time. God used you to get his attention."

"So, y'all really gon' talk about me like I ain't standing here?" Dro asked.

"That's how they do men in this house," Lenny said, stepping into the kitchen. "Hey, son. Good to see you."

"'Sup, Pop?" Dro smiled, as the men shook hands. "This is Forever. Forever, this Pops."

"Hey, Forever. It's a pleasure to meet you."

"Hi, Mr. Williams. It's nice to meet you, too."

"It's Lenny. We don't do formalities in this house."

"Okay, Lenny."

Lenny gave Dro a nudge. "You did good with this one, son. See my good taste in women rubbed off on you."

"Yeah, Pop. You did alright for yourself by marrying Marcia," Dro cracked.

"Call me Marcia again and I'ma act like Forever ain't standing here and go get my belt. You ain't too old to get yo' butt whooped."

"C'mon, Mama. You know you my girl. Why you wanna do yo' boy like that?" Dro said, giving his mother another hug.

Forever loved the way Dro interacted with his family. The house was filled with genuine love, and she could feel it.

"Okay, son. What do you say about grabbing some beers and going to watch this Bucks game? They playing Golden State, and it's halftime. Giannis about to get another triple double."

Dro turned to Forever. "You good in here?"

Marcia waved him off. "Boy, we ain't gon' bite her. Get out of my kitchen."

"Now that they gone, we can get down to business," Shanice smiled. "How did you and my brother meet? You know he crazy, right?"

Marcia cut her eyes at Shanice. "Stop it. Ruben is a good young man, Forever. He just had to figure some things out on his own time."

"I know. I really like him. He has a good heart."

"He was raised the right way. Somehow he picked up his daddy's knack for getting in trouble. Can you cook?"

She looked uncomfortable. "Um. A little."

"Everything is done now. I just need you to grab some ice cream out the freezer and a scooper out the drawer. Put two scoops in some bowls for me. Bowls in the cabinet behind you. Then put them in the freezer."

When everyone went back to their cooking assignments, Shanice got nosey again. "Seriously though, Forever. How did you and my brother meet?"

Not wanting to tell his family she ran him over, she told a half-truth. "We had a car accident."

"I heard you ran him over."

Forever laughed. "I did. It was an accident."

"Sounds like you knocked some sense into him," Marcia laughed.

"Yeah, I might've."

"Well, I want you to know I think you're good for him. He's about to start a business and ain't running the streets at all times of the night doing Lord knows what. I know a woman can't teach a man how to be a man, but we possess wisdom and insights into their souls and can point out things they might not be aware of. Thank you for whatever you pointed out to him that helped him get his head on right."

Forever was touched by the heartfelt words. "I don't know what to say. I just like him so much, and I seen his potential. And I wanted to help him fulfill the calling the preacher said he had."

"A preacher prophesied over Ruben?" Kailah asked, appearing out of nowhere.

"Yes. When he was little. Before you were born," Marcia explained.

"He actually used to go to church?" Kailah scoffed. "I'm surprised that little devil didn't catch on fire."

***

"I'm so in love with your family," Forever gushed from the passenger seat of the Corvette.

"Yeah, they a'ight. And they crazy about you, too. And I think Lenny crushing on you."

"No, he's not!" she laughed. "But being around them makes me wish I had that kind of family atmosphere growing up. Whenever I have kids, I want to raise them in that kind of environment."

Dro took his eyes off the road to glance at her. "We finna talk about kids? For real?"

"Ruben, stop playing. We're not having any kids. At least not until we get married. Speaking of kids, when am I going to get to meet the other lady in your life?"

"I'm going to arrange that soon. You'll love her. That's my baby."

"I can't wait," she said, then remembered something. "Hey, why were you acting funny earlier when I asked you about your car?"

He went stiff again. "What you talking about?"

"I'm talking about what you just did. Getting all uptight. What happened?"

He was quiet for a moment before letting out a long breath. "I got shot at earlier."

Forever became hysterical. "What? Are you serious? Are you okay? What happened?"

"I'm good. My car got shot up."

"Why didn't you tell me?"

"Because I didn't want you to worry."

"But we're in a relationship now. We're getting closer. I'm your woman. You have to tell me stuff like this. Don't you trust me?"

"I do trust you, baby. I didn't get hurt, and I didn't want you to worry."

"If I want to be worried, let me be worried. You can't keep things like that from me if our relationship is to be based on trust."

"You right. My bad. I was just trying to protect you."

"I'm not the one who needs protecting. Do you know who did it?"

"Nah. And I don't care. I went to the hood to talk to the Savages when it happened. I was about to tell them I was leaving the clique when somebody started shooting."

"Do you want to move out of Milwaukee?"

"Nah. I ain't runnin' from nobody. I'm good."

She got mad. "Why not? You made a lot of enemies here. People are trying to kill you. I don't want anything to happen to you."

"I'm good. This is why I didn't want to tell you. Let's just leave it alone for right now. We'll talk about it later when we calm down."

She gave him a long stare before turning to look out the window.

***

Ruben sat on the edge of the seat, unable to take his eyes off Pastor McClain. Sweat glistened on the preacher's forehead, running down the sides of his face and dripping onto his suit. He grabbed a white hand towel from the podium to wipe away the perspiration for the hundredth time. The sweat disappeared only to return a few moments later.

"Now, I'm going to tell you something, church. Beware of those that laugh at your seed, but want to eat your harvest. They make fun of your dreams, but got they hand out when it comes to life. Can I get an Amen?"

The church erupted with Amens.

"There are times when you have to make a decision in life. Do you plant that little mustard seed of faith and do what needs to be done to reap a bountiful harvest a hundred times over? Or do you let the people who laugh at the size of your seed ridicule you for missing the mark and dump their worldly cares upon you that cause you not to take a step forward in faith? Am I talking to somebody this morning?"

The preacher's question jarred something inside of Dro, making him reflect and soul search. It was as if everything he had gone through for the last couple of months had led him to this moment. To this event. To this place. And he asked himself if he was ready to plant that seed.

"God told me to tell somebody that the time is now. Discipline is the fuel of achievement, and you will either suffer the pain of discipline or the pain of regret. Pick a side. God is calling somebody right now. The Holy Spirit is nudging you on. And if I'm talking to you and you ready to step out on faith, I want you to come up here right now and stand behind me on this platform."

Behind Pastor McClain was a giant swimming pool half-filled with water. Surrounding the pool were members of the church holding towels and robes.

"That's right, church. If you need forgiveness, come on up here. If you tired of being sick and tired, c'mon up. If you need a blessing, c'mon up. If you need God to show up in your life, c'mon. Obey the Lord, y'all. Come up here and receive what the Lord has for you."

When the choir began singing, people began to get up slowly from their seats, moving to the front of the church. Men, women, boys, and girls. Dro felt something tugging on the inside, urging him to follow the people up to the pool. But he resisted, worried about how people would look at him for being a Christian. He didn't want to look like a fool or be judged if he couldn't live up to the standards of being saved.

But something kept pulling him, and the pastor's words grew louder in his head. Then, before he knew it, he was on his feet, moving toward the front of the church. When he got to the platform, he formed a circle around the pool with the rest of the parishioners who wanted to receive what God was giving. An assistant pastor walked around with a bottle of oil, anointing their foreheads and praying while a deacon had them remove the items from their pockets. Then, one by one, all of them were dipped in the pool and baptized in the name of Jesus.

When Dro came out of the water, it felt as if he left all his burdens in the pool. Spiritually, he felt brand new. The guilt was lifted from his heart, and for the first time in a long time, he felt free.

***

"I can't even explain what was happening to me when I was walking down that aisle. It was like something took control of me. Like my body was moving by itself," Dro explained.

He was at A Taste of Manna, a soul food restaurant owned by a member of the church. Forever, Sasha, and her boyfriend were tucked away in the booth with him, eating brunch.

"You should've seen Forever, Ruben. She was crying like she was at a funeral," Sasha laughed.

"And then, by some act of God, she was out of her seat and up on that platform before you even got out the water," Stanley added. "At first I thought she caught the Holy Ghost."

"Surprised me, too," Dro chuckled. "Almost knocked me down when she ran up there and hugged me."

"C'mon, y'all," Forever blushed. "You two don't know where he came from. It's amazing watching God work in his life. I was caught up in the presence of God."

Dro smiled proudly, happy he could share the moment with his girl. "I know, baby. I felt it, too. I'm glad you was there with me."

"Aw! That's so sweet!" Sasha gushed. "Y'all look so good together. Y'all gon' have pretty babies."

"Young Dro!"

Dro's body went stiff at the sound of the voice. He couldn't believe Lunatic was at the restaurant. And if Luna was here, that meant the rest of the Savages were close. Even though they were his day-ones, he didn't want to see them right now. Not after being baptized and being out with people from church.

"Dro, I know you heard me callin' you, nigga!"

He still hadn't spun around, but the looks on Sasha, Stanley, and Forever's faces let him know more than one person was approaching.

When Dro finally spun around, the Savages were a few feet away. "What y'all doin' in here?" he asked.

"Shit," Tae grinned. "Came in this bitch to get somethin' to eat. Heard they shit bangin'."

"What you doin' in here? Who this?" Twenty asked, eyeing Sasha and Forever while ignoring Stanley.

Dro stood, attempting to lead his niggas away from the table. "These my people. Where y'all sittin' at?"

"Way over there," Luna pointed to the other side of the restaurant. "We seen you and came over."

"Let's go over there. Forever, y'all go ahead without me. I gotta take care of something."

"Ruben, wait!" Forever called.

"I'm good. Go 'head," he said before walking away.

"Who them hos?" Twenty asked, looking back.

"And what up wit' this suit? You in a band, nigga?" Tae cracked.

"I just came from church. Them females part of the church."

Twenty and Tae exchanged glances. "Dawg, you serious? You on this churchy shit, for real?" Tae asked.

"C'mon, nigga. Y'all knew I grew up going to church."

"I know. Shit, we all went to church when we was shorties. This what you on now? I knew you watched preachers on TV, but I didn't know how serious you was."

After they had seats, Dro told them what was on his chest. "Listen, y'all. The sun don't shine forever. I got a hunnit Gs, and I wanna be around long enough to spend it."

"Oh, this nigga serious?" Twenty asked.

Dro nodded.

"So, that's why you ain't been in the hood? You 'bout to leave the squad?"

Dro nodded again, glancing toward Forever. She was gathering her things. They locked eyes for a moment, concern reflecting in her irises.

"I gotta walk away from this shit, my nigga. Gotta think about more than just me. I gotta daughter. How much longer y'all think we can make it taking niggas' shit? We got enemies all over the city. I got popped twice and went to jail too many times. I wanna walk away by choice, not because I'm forced. I ain't trynna get life or die."

Tae looked at Dro like he sold out.

Twenty ran his hands over his face and let out a long breath. "First Luna was talkin' that shit, now you. This shit don't even seem real."

"I feel 'im," Lunatic spoke up. "What more do niggas need? We just hit for seventy-five. I know you niggas ain't finna blow it on bullshit and be robbing niggas again in a couple days. Dro right. He finna start a business and flip the script. Shit, once I get these charges behind me, I'm hittin' the ATL. We gon' always be Savages, but niggas tired of gettin' shot and goin' to jail. It's time to get money and live."

"That shit sound soft as a bitch," Tae spat. "I hear you niggas on making money, but I'm out here. Fuck what you heard."

"Why you always gotta say some bullshit, nigga?" Dro mugged.

"Ain't nobody disrespectin' you, nigga. I'm speaking my mind," he said before looking behind Dro.

Forever walked up. "Ruben, can I talk to you for a moment?"

He spun to face her, a serious look on his face. "I'ma catch you later."

"But, Ruben, I need to talk to –"

"Not right now. I'm good. Trust me."

After a short, angry staredown, she let out a frustrated noise before spinning on her heels and walking away.

"Damn, she bad!" Tae said. "Who is she?"

"Look at that ass!" Twenty added. "You hit that?"

"That's my girl, Forever."

"Yo' main bitch?" Tae asked, wanting clarity.

"My only."

Tae laughed. "Oh! So that's why you gettin' on this new shit. Get some new pussy and flip the script."

Dro wanted to bust Tae in his shit again, but held his composure.

"Chill, Tae," Twenty said. "Sound like the nigga gave it some thought. Damn, my nigga. I hate to see you niggas go, but I understand."

"You know y'all always gon' be my niggas. We grew up and threw up together. But we got a lil'lil' money now. We got our own cribs and whips. We good. What more is out here?"

"This all I know, my nigga," Tae said. "If you and Luna wanna get on some otha shit, I'm cool wit' it. Y'all still my niggas. But I'm dying a street nigga. This shit in me, fam. I bought some work and put some lil'lil' niggas on. That's how I'ma make my money. But, y'all do y'all. It's all love."

"What I tell you, Dro?" Lunatic laughed. "Niggas eat gun powder and shit bullets."

The Savages shared a laugh, easing some of the tension.

"Whatever happened with Rich Boy and Trouble?" Dro asked.

"Rich Boy got his shit splattered on the sidewalk. Trouble in a wheelchair," Tae said.

"Ain't no tellin' who did that shit, either," Twenty said. "Niggas done did so much dirt. But as soon as I hear who did it, I'm in them niggas' asses."

"Would you gentlemen like to place an order?" a waitress asked, walking up to the table.

Lunatic picked up the menu. "Hell yeah. I'm hungry as fuck. What's the special?"

194

After having a meal, they hopped in Tae's Tahoe to drive Dro home. During the ride, he thought of everything he'd been through with the Savages. Fights, shootings, shootouts, orgies, drug deals, jail. A piece of his life would be missing after he left them behind. When Tae pulled up to his house, he almost didn't want to get out of the car.

"A'ight, nigga. Getcho square ass out," Tae smiled, turning to face Dro.

"And don't be no stranger, nigga," Twenty said. "This Savage shit ain't no t-shirt or tat. This in our blood."

"And since you done smoking and drinking, make sure you call me to come get that paraphernalia. I know you keep that good shit." Lunatic laughed.

"I ain't gon' be no stranger. And I'm still smoking weed. God made plants. I love you niggas. Stay dangerous."

"You know I will," Tae chuckled. "Savage."

Getting out of the truck felt like a funeral. The old him was dead and gone. Just like he left the burdens in the water when he got baptized, he left the old him in the back seat of Tae's truck.

As soon as he got in the house, he called Forever. "Where are you?" she answered.

"I just walked through my front door."

"Are you okay? Who were those guys?"

"Them was my boys. The Savages. I told them I was out."

She let out a sigh of relief. "I was so worried. I didn't know what was going on."

He laughed. "I'm good, baby. I told you I had it. You gotta trust me, too."

"You're right. And I'm proud of you for telling them you are leaving. I know it wasn't easy. You have to accept what is, let go of what was, and have faith in what will be."

"Damn, that was deep, baby. Where you get that?"

"It was in my daily devotional this morning. I didn't know what it meant 'til just now."

"Well, I got one for you. You may only be someone in this world, but to someone else, you may be the world."

Forever burst out laughing. "You can't one-up me. Mine was way better."

"Whatever. I know mine was better. Where you at?"

"Turning onto your street. Open the door."

Chapter 18

"Good morning, sir. How may I help you?"

Dro eyed the short Mexican woman's name tag. "Hey, Alana. I'm looking for Forever Mitchell."

She eyed him and his guest. "And you are?"

"I'm Ruben, and this is my daughter, Asia. We're surprising her for lunch. Can you keep it hush until she come?"

"Awe, this is so sweet!" She melted, picking up the phone. "Wait one moment while I call her office."

While she made the call, Dro looked around the Social Services Building. It was huge, and people in suits and professional dress moved around with lightening speed, like they were all in a race.

"She'll be down in one moment, sir. You and your daughter can have seats. I didn't tell her who you were, just that she had a visitor."

"Okay. Thanks," Dro said before leading Asia to the sitting area.

"Why couldn't I bring Scooter, Daddy?" his daughter asked.

"'Cause, for the millionth time, that dog ain't riding in my car no more."

"Why not? How come your friends can ride in it but my friend can't?"

"My car, my rules. Plus, my friends are human and don't use the bathroom on the seats."

"It only happened one time, Daddy," she giggled. "He knows better now."

"So do I. That's why he ain't riding with me no more."

"You are a party pooper, Daddy. This ain't fair."

"Well, get your own car."

"I am. As soon as I turn sixteen. And I'm not letting you get in it."

Dro looked down at her poked-out lip and couldn't help but laugh. Even when she was sad, she was still cute.

"Ruben! Hey. What are you doing here?" Forever asked, walking into the sitting area. When she seen Asia, her eyes popped. "Is that who I think it is?"

Dro stood to hug her. "Hey, baby. This is my other baby, Asia. Asia, this is Forever."

"Oh, my goodness! She is so pretty. Hi, Asia!"

"Hi," she waved, acting shy.

"I've been waiting to meet you for a long time. How are you doing?"

"Fine."

"She is adorable," Forever said, turning back to Dro. "What are you guys doing here?"

"We came to surprise you, hoping to steal you away for the rest of the day."

Forever looked upset. "Ruben, why didn't you tell me this morning? I could've taken the day off."

"Something came up with her mom. Since I have her for the day, I wanted to stop by."

Before Forever could answer, a short, white woman with brown hair called her name. "Hey, Forever?"

She turned and saw a coworker walking over. "Hi, Nancy."

"Hey. I was just on my way to your office to see if you wanted to do lunch, but I can see you're with clients. Will you be free later?"

"No, these aren't clients. This is my boyfriend, Ruben, and his daughter, Asia. Ruben, this is Nancy."

He extended a hand. "Nice to meet you, Nancy."

The white woman sized him up. "So, you're Ruben, huh? I've heard a lot about you."

"Hopefully it was good," he said, giving Forever a look.

"It was great. You're everything I expected. So, what brings you guys here?"

Dro glanced at Forever, surprised by her coworker's boldness. Forever responded by shooting eye daggers at Nancy that she didn't care to acknowledge. Instead, she watched Dro expectantly, waiting for him to answer her question.

"I came to steal your friend for the rest of the day, but it looks like that might not be happening."

Nancy looked surprised. "Why not?"

"It's a bad time," Forever cut in. "I have to deal with the Johnson file, and I have a bunch of cases that –"

"Nonsense," Nancy waved. "Get out of here. I'll cover for you."

"C'mon, Nancy. You don't even know the case. I don't want you to –"

"I said go. I'll handle it. Trust me. Get out of here. Can't leave this tall, dark, and handsome man alone," she winked.

Forever smiled, revealing how badly she wanted to leave in her eyes. "Thank you so much, Nancy. I owe you big time."

From Forever's job, Dro drove to the state fair. He was surprised at how well Asia and his girl got along, considering his daughter wanted him to get back with America so they could be a family. But things were going smoothly, and he felt at peace.

They had just walked past a concession stand when Asia's eyes threatened to pop out of her head. "Ooh! Daddy, can you win me a big bear?"

"You know I got you, baby," Dro said, stopping to look at the game and prizes. It was a basketball game. Ten rims spaced apart. The further the shot, the better the prize.

"Are you sure you're ready for this, Mr. I-Sprained-My-Wrist?" Forever laughed, holding two big, pink flamingos.

"I got you that bird, didn't I?" he asked, pulling out money and walking up to the counter.

"Yeah. After twenty tries. I won Asia the other one in only three."

"I told you, I sprained my wrist. Plus, baseball ain't my sport. I grew up hooping. I ain't never met nobody from the hood that couldn't play ball. Watch this," he said, paying for five shots.

"Okay, LeBron James."

"Watch yo' mouth, girl!" he mugged. "This about the Greek Freak," he said before chucking the first shot.

Missed wide right.

"Get it closer, Daddy," Asia said.

"You look rusty, Mr. Freak," Forever teased.

"Keep laughing. Bet I won't miss this one," he said before taking another shot.

Missed again.

"Hold these, Asia," Forever said, giving her the flamingos. "Let me try, baby."

"Nah, nah. You bad luck. Get away from me. You come stand next to me, Asia. As soon as I get ready to shoot, say Giannis."

When his daughter stood next to him, he gave her a nod.

"Giannis!" she yelled.

The net swished and he held his hand in the air for effect, sticking out his tongue at Forever. "Say something now. Yo, my man. Gimme that big brown bear," Dro told the man behind the counter.

Forever pushed him out of the way. "Move. It's my turn."

"You don't know nothing about hoops," he laughed. "You was too busy in dance recitals and wearing pink tutus."

She gave him a look. "I'm going to tell you something you don't know about me, Ruben. We were runner-up at state during my sophomore year in high school. I was the starting point guard," she said before launching a ball.

Nothing but net.

"Yeah, Forever! Girl power!" Asia cheered, giving her a high five.

"Traitor," Dro mumbled, snatching the bear he won from Asia.

"Gimme my bear back, Daddy!"

"Nah, this my bear. I won it," he teased.

"That's okay. Let him keep it," Forever said. "You can have the bear I just won."

"Ruben!" someone called from behind them.

He turned and seen an older, light-skinned lady walking toward him wearing a smile. She was flanked by two women in their early twenties.

"Aunty Candice! What up?" Dro grinned. "Hey, Savannah. What up, Kathy?"

"Hey, Savannah and Kathy!" Asia waved to her cousins.

"I thought that was you," Candice smiled. "I haven't seen you in a long time. How is the family?"

"Everybody doin' good. This is my girlfriend, Forever. Baby, this is my aunt Candice and her daughters, Savannah and Kathy."

The women exchanged pleasantries.

"How is your uncle? Have you seen him lately?"

Dro thought about Crush's living arrangements. "It's been a little while. He's making it, I guess. Still hanging in there."

The eyes of the mother and daughters reflected emotions and words that didn't need to be spoken to be understood. "Next time you see him, tell him I hope he gets himself together one day."

He was about to respond when he seen a face in the crowd that made every nerve in his body tingle. Dark skin, fishlike eyes, and a scar on the right side of the face. He noticed Dro at the same time, locking eyes briefly before looking away.

"Okay, I will. It was nice seeing y'all. I gotta get Asia home," Dro said, eyeing the man until he disappeared in the crowd.

"Okay. Take care. Tell your mother I'm going to the next family reunion. We had a good time at the last one."

"C'mon, y'all. Let's go," Dro said, grabbing Asia's hand.

"Wait, Daddy! I wanna ride the Spin-O-Rama," Asia protested.

"Not today, baby girl," Dro said, searching the crowd for the nigga with the scar. "I'ma make it up to you with some dessert. Let's get some ice cream cake."

"You okay?" Forever asked, noticing he was acting funny.

He tried to play it cool. "Yeah. I'm good. I thought I seen somebody I –" He stopped talking when he realized how he knew the nigga with the scar. It was Tulip's baby daddy.

"What, Daddy?" Asia asked.

"Yeah, what were you about to say?" Forever asked.

He didn't want to say too much around Asia, but he needed to let Forever know the situation was serious. "I seen somebody I used to know, and I don't want them to see me."

She quickly understood what he meant and looked for the exit. "Oh, yeah! I want to taste that ice cream cake, too. Double chocolate."

They took a few steps when J-Mac popped up in front of them. And he wasn't alone. His two niggas were mugging. Everyone stopped and had a staredown. Dro knew what was about to happen.

"Hey, Ruben! One more thing," Savannah called, walking over. She immediately noticed the hostility between J-Mac and company.

"Y'all go that way!" Dro said, using his body to shield his ladies. When he looked back, J-Mac and his niggas went for their waists.

"Shit! Run!"

Pop-pop-pop-pop-pop-pop-pop-pop-pop-pop!

Boom, boom, boom, boom, boom, boom, boom!

"Ah, shit!" Dro screamed as bullets tore into his back and legs. He fell to the ground face-first.

The people at the state fair screamed, running away. Those who didn't move fast enough were cut down by the gunfire.

The shooting was over as quickly as it started, and bodies were strewn all over the ground. He looked for Asia and Forever. They lay on the ground a few feet away, next to Savannah. The worst pain he'd ever felt hit him in the chest. It felt worse than the bullets in his back.

"No! Hell nah!" he cursed, struggling to stand. The bullets in his legs wouldn't allow it, so he began crawling.

The closer he got, the more he could see how bad the situation was. Blood spots were on Forever's back. Asia and Savannah weren't moving.

"Asia? Forever! Y'all good?"

Forever grunted, trying to sit up. "Ruben! Where are you? I'm shot, baby!"

"I'm right here. Ah, shit. I'm shot, too. Asia, you okay, baby? Get up. Talk to me, baby girl."

The little girl didn't move, and blood covered the back of her head. The sight made a part of his soul go dark.

To Be Continued…
The Savage Life 2
Coming Soon

Submission Guideline

Submit the first three chapters of your completed manuscript to ldpsubmissions@gmail.com, subject line: Your book's title. The manuscript must be in a .doc file and sent as an attachment. Document should be in Times New Roman, double spaced and in size 12 font. Also, provide your synopsis and full contact information. If sending multiple submissions, they must each be in a separate email.

Have a story but no way to send it electronically? You can still submit to LDP/Ca$h Presents. Send in the first three chapters, written or typed, of your completed manuscript to:

LDP: Submissions Dept
Po Box 870494
Mesquite, Tx 75187

DO NOT send original manuscript. Must be a duplicate.

Provide your synopsis and a cover letter containing your full contact information.

Thanks for considering LDP and Ca$h Presents.

J-Blunt

Coming Soon from Lock Down Publications/Ca$h Presents

BOW DOWN TO MY GANGSTA

By **Ca$h**

TORN BETWEEN TWO

By **Coffee**

BLOOD STAINS OF A SHOTTA **III**

By **Jamaica**

STEADY MOBBIN **III**

By **Marcellus Allen**

RENEGADE BOYS IV

By Meesha

BLOOD OF A BOSS **VI**

SHADOWS OF THE GAME II

By **Askari**

LOYAL TO THE GAME **IV**

LIFE OF SIN **III**

By **T.J. & Jelissa**

A DOPEBOY'S PRAYER **II**

By **Eddie "Wolf" Lee**

IF LOVING YOU IS WRONG… **III**

By **Jelissa**

TRUE SAVAGE **VII**

By **Chris Green**

BLAST FOR ME **III**

DUFFLE BAG CARTEL **IV**

HEARTLESS GOON **II**

The Savage Life

By **Ghost**
A HUSTLER'S DECEIT III
KILL ZONE **II**
BAE BELONGS TO ME III
SOUL OF A MONSTER III
By **Aryanna**
THE COST OF LOYALTY **III**
By **Kweli**
A GANGSTER'S SYN III
THE SAVAGE LIFE II
By **J-Blunt**
KING OF NEW YORK V
RISE TO POWER III
COKE KINGS IV
BORN HEARTLESS II
By **T.J. Edwards**
GORILLAZ IN THE BAY IV
De'Kari
THE STREETS ARE CALLING II
Duquie Wilson
KINGPIN KILLAZ IV
STREET KINGS III
PAID IN BLOOD II
Hood Rich
SINS OF A HUSTLA II
ASAD
TRIGGADALE III

Elijah R. Freeman

KINGZ OF THE GAME IV

Playa Ray

SLAUGHTER GANG IV

RUTHLESS HEART

By Willie Slaughter

THE HEART OF A SAVAGE II

By Jibril Williams

FUK SHYT II

By Blakk Diamond

THE DOPEMAN'S BODYGAURD II

By Tranay Adams

TRAP GOD

By Troublesome

YAYO II

By S. Allen

GHOST MOB

Stilloan Robinson

KINGPIN DREAMS

By Paper Boi Rari

CREAM

By Yolanda Moore

Available Now

RESTRAINING ORDER **I & II**

By **CA$H & Coffee**

LOVE KNOWS NO BOUNDARIES **I II & III**

By **Coffee**

RAISED AS A GOON I, II, III & IV

BRED BY THE SLUMS I, II, III

BLAST FOR ME I & II

ROTTEN TO THE CORE I II III

A BRONX TALE I, II, III

DUFFEL BAG CARTEL I II III

HEARTLESS GOON

A SAVAGE DOPEBOY

HEARTLESS GOON

By **Ghost**

LAY IT DOWN **I & II**

LAST OF A DYING BREED

BLOOD STAINS OF A SHOTTA I & II

By **Jamaica**

LOYAL TO THE GAME

LOYAL TO THE GAME II

LOYAL TO THE GAME III

LIFE OF SIN I, II

By **TJ & Jelissa**

BLOODY COMMAS I & II

SKI MASK CARTEL I II & III

KING OF NEW YORK I II,III IV

RISE TO POWER I II

J-Blunt

COKE KINGS I II III

BORN HEARTLESS

By **T.J. Edwards**

IF LOVING HIM IS WRONG…I & II

LOVE ME EVEN WHEN IT HURTS I II III

By **Jelissa**

WHEN THE STREETS CLAP BACK I & II III

By **Jibril Williams**

A DISTINGUISHED THUG STOLE MY HEART I II & III

LOVE SHOULDN'T HURT I II III IV

RENEGADE BOYS I II III

By **Meesha**

A GANGSTER'S CODE I &, II III

A GANGSTER'S SYN I II

THE SAVAGE LIFE

By **J-Blunt**

PUSH IT TO THE LIMIT

By **Bre' Hayes**

BLOOD OF A BOSS **I, II, III, IV, V**

SHADOWS OF THE GAME

By **Askari**

THE STREETS BLEED MURDER **I, II & III**

THE HEART OF A GANGSTA I II& III

By **Jerry Jackson**

CUM FOR ME

CUM FOR ME 2

CUM FOR ME 3

CUM FOR ME 4

CUM FOR ME 5

An **LDP Erotica Collaboration**

BRIDE OF A HUSTLA **I II & II**

THE FETTI GIRLS **I, II& III**

CORRUPTED BY A GANGSTA I, II III, IV

BLINDED BY HIS LOVE

By **Destiny Skai**

WHEN A GOOD GIRL GOES BAD

By **Adrienne**

THE COST OF LOYALTY I II

By Kweli

A GANGSTER'S REVENGE **I II III & IV**

THE BOSS MAN'S DAUGHTERS

THE BOSS MAN'S DAUGHTERS II

THE BOSSMAN'S DAUGHTERS III

THE BOSSMAN'S DAUGHTERS IV

THE BOSS MAN'S DAUGHTERS **V**

A SAVAGE LOVE **I & II**

BAE BELONGS TO ME I II

A HUSTLER'S DECEIT I, II, III

WHAT BAD BITCHES DO I, II, III

SOUL OF A MONSTER I II

KILL ZONE

By **Aryanna**

A KINGPIN'S AMBITON

A KINGPIN'S AMBITION **II**

I MURDER FOR THE DOUGH

By **Ambitious**

TRUE SAVAGE

TRUE SAVAGE II

TRUE SAVAGE **III**

TRUE SAVAGE **IV**

TRUE SAVAGE **V**

TRUE SAVAGE **VI**

By **Chris Green**

A DOPEBOY'S PRAYER

By **Eddie "Wolf" Lee**

THE KING CARTEL **I, II & III**

By **Frank Gresham**

THESE NIGGAS AIN'T LOYAL **I, II & III**

By **Nikki Tee**

GANGSTA SHYT **I II &III**

By **CATO**

THE ULTIMATE BETRAYAL

By **Phoenix**

BOSS'N UP **I , II & III**

By **Royal Nicole**

I LOVE YOU TO DEATH

By Destiny J

I RIDE FOR MY HITTA

I STILL RIDE FOR MY HITTA

By **Misty Holt**

LOVE & CHASIN' PAPER

By **Qay Crockett**

TO DIE IN VAIN

SINS OF A HUSTLA

By **ASAD**

BROOKLYN HUSTLAZ

By **Boogsy Morina**

BROOKLYN ON LOCK I & II

By **Sonovia**

GANGSTA CITY

By **Teddy Duke**

A DRUG KING AND HIS DIAMOND I & II III

A DOPEMAN'S RICHES

HER MAN, MINE'S TOO I, II

CASH MONEY HO'S

By Nicole Goosby

TRAPHOUSE KING **I II & III**

KINGPIN KILLAZ I II III

STREET KINGS I II

PAID IN BLOOD

By **Hood Rich**

LIPSTICK KILLAH **I, II, III**

CRIME OF PASSION I & II

By **Mimi**

STEADY MOBBN' **I, II, III**

By **Marcellus Allen**

WHO SHOT YA **I, II, III**

Renta

J-Blunt

GORILLAZ IN THE BAY **I II III**

DE'KARI

TRIGGADALE I II

Elijah R. Freeman

GOD BLESS THE TRAPPERS I, II, III

THESE SCANDALOUS STREETS I, II, III

FEAR MY GANGSTA I, II, III

THESE STREETS DON'T LOVE NOBODY I, II

BURY ME A G I, II, III, IV, V

A GANGSTA'S EMPIRE I, II, III, IV

THE DOPEMAN'S BODYGAURD

Tranay Adams

THE STREETS ARE CALLING

Duquie Wilson

MARRIED TO A BOSS... I II III

By Destiny Skai & Chris Green

KINGZ OF THE GAME I II III

Playa Ray

SLAUGHTER GANG I II III

By Willie Slaughter

THE HEART OF A SAVAGE

By Jibril Williams

FUK SHYT

By Blakk Diamond

DON'T F#CK WITH MY HEART I II

By Linnea

ADDICTED TO THE DRAMA I II III

214

The Savage Life

By Jamila

YAYO

By S. Allen

BOOKS BY LDP'S CEO, CA$H

TRUST IN NO MAN

TRUST IN NO MAN 2

TRUST IN NO MAN 3

BONDED BY BLOOD

SHORTY GOT A THUG

THUGS CRY

THUGS CRY 2

THUGS CRY 3

TRUST NO BITCH

TRUST NO BITCH 2

TRUST NO BITCH 3

TIL MY CASKET DROPS

RESTRAINING ORDER

RESTRAINING ORDER 2

IN LOVE WITH A CONVICT

Coming Soon

BONDED BY BLOOD 2

BOW DOWN TO MY GANGSTA